A FIGHTING CHANCE

White Dove Romances

9612

A FIGHTING CHANCE

YVONNE LEHMAN

BETHANY HOUSE PUBLISHERS
MINNEAPOLIS, MINNESOTA 55438

A Fighting Chance
Copyright © 1997
Yvonne Lehman

Cover by Peter Glöege

Published by Bethany House Publishers
A Ministry of Bethany Fellowship, Inc.
11300 Hampshire Avenue South
Minneapolis, Minnesota 55438

Printed in the United States of America.

Library of Congress Cataloging-in-Publication Data

Lehman, Yvonne.
    A fighting chance / by Yvonne Lehman.
        p. cm. — (A white dove romance ; book #5)
    Summary: When her boyfriend Sean's mood swings and
abusive behavior threaten to end their relationship, seventeen-
year-old Ruthie blames herself for Sean's turning away from
God.
    ISBN 1-55661-709-7 (pbk.)
        [1. Christian life—Fiction. 2. Interpersonal relations—
Fiction. 3. Dating violence—Fiction.] I. Title. II. Series:
Lehman, Yvonne. White dove romances ; 5.
PZ7.L5322Fi   1997
[Fic]—dc21   97–4709
                                                      CIP
                                                      AC

To those whose help and
encouragement are invaluable:

Lori,
Anne,
Rochelle,
Howard.

YVONNE LEHMAN is the award-winning author of eighteen published novels, including ten inspirational romances, two contemporary novels, a biblical novel, *In Shady Groves*, and five young adult novels. She and her husband, Howard, have four grown children and five grandchildren, and they make their home in the mountains of North Carolina.

We say:
"Sticks and stones may break my bones,
but words will never harm me."

The Bible says:
"Put on the full armor of God, so that when the day
of evil comes, you may be able to stand your
ground. . . . Take . . . the sword of the Spirit,
which is the word of God."

—Ephesians 6:13, 17

One

He's in a rotten mood again! Ruthie Ryan thought the moment she opened the car door and caught a glimpse of Sean Jacson's face, as stormy as the low-hanging clouds threatening to dump a winter mix on Garden City. At least that's what the TV weatherman had called it. But here in southern Illinois, "winter mix" could mean anything from a blizzard to an ice storm.

She jumped into the passenger seat and slammed the door shut.

"Don't tear it off the hinges," Sean growled.

She shot him an inquisitive look. "Well, sorry. I'm just glad to see you, that's all." Was that ever the truth! She and her boyfriend hadn't been spending much time together now that Sean worked evenings and weekends at Little Egypt Supermarket Warehouse.

Taking another glance in his direction, she noticed that his face had thinned out a little. But that only brought out his great cheekbones, and with that tan and his blond hair—worn longer, now that he'd given up football—wow! No wonder she was crazy about him.

9

Laying her hand on his shoulder affectionately, Ruthie leaned over, her face close to his. Sean didn't turn toward her, so her kiss landed on his cheek.

"Whoa! Your lips are cold," he complained, wiping off the kiss with one hand.

Ruthie bit back the retort that almost slipped out. *Not as cold as your attitude, big guy! And maybe if you kissed me back, that would warm them up!* But Sean didn't need any smart remarks. His life was the pits now that his mom and dad were separated and getting a divorce.

"Just trying to cheer you up," she said, with less bounce in her comment than in the coils of rust-colored curls framing her face. Retreating to her side of the car, she slumped into her seat—the atmosphere as chilly as the skiff of snow that had fallen on Garden City overnight. Outside the window, evergreens and grass were frosted with white, and there were patches of ice on the road. Shivering, Ruthie hugged her arms. The heater in Sean's old plug wasn't putting out any more warmth than *he* was.

"So . . . cheer me up," Sean said bitingly, his gray-green eyes vacant as they began to chug up the street. "Get me a new car—or at least one that works. Make my mom and dad stop fighting. Give me time to do my homework. Oh yeah, and how about a pile of money so I don't have to break my back at that warehouse! Mom doesn't make enough to pay the bills. And Dad doesn't have any extra now that he's got his own place."

When Sean had unloaded, Ruthie cut her eyes around at him. "I was just thinking. . . . Your mom's a single parent now, and with Christmas coming, I hear the youth group at church is thinking about filling some boxes with food and stuff. Do you think . . . I mean . . . would you want us to—?"

She broke off the minute she caught his angry glare. His eyes bore a hole into hers. He stared so long she was afraid he was going to run off the road.

"Don't . . . even . . . *think* it." His icy tone was ten times worse than a shout. "We Jacsons—at least, Mom and I—are not some charity case. I'd quit school and take *two* jobs before I'd take a handout."

"Sorry." She looked away from that laserlike gaze. "Nothing wrong with accepting a little help when you need it," she mumbled under her breath. Then, "We took some boxes of food to Stephanie and Andy that time, remember?"

"That's different. The Kellys are the youth directors at church." He shrugged, concentrating on the road. "But my dad never went to church . . . and Mom's too tired on the weekends to go."

Might help if they did! flashed through Ruthie's mind. But she'd better not put her foot in it with a remark like that.

Normally, by this time she would have snapped off some kind of verbal jab like "Stop feeling sorry for yourself, Sean." But that was no solution, either. Didn't the Bible say something about the tongue being like a sharp sword? Sometimes Sean's cutting remarks practically drew blood!

She searched for a topic that wouldn't set him off, but before she could come up with anything, he was pulling into the church parking lot, only a few blocks from her house. To her surprise, he didn't park, but stopped at the side door and left the engine running.

"I'm not staying, Ruthie," he said bluntly.

She stared at him, open-mouthed. "Why not? I thought you had the night off."

"I just don't feel like it. Why don't we"—he spread his hands—"go to the Pizza Palace and talk."

"About what?"

"Just . . . stuff." He braced his arms on the steering wheel and studied his thumbs. "I really need you, Ruthie. Nobody else listens to me."

"Well . . ." The idea was tempting. Time alone with Sean. . . . "I'd have to call my parents first."

"Oh, come on, Ruthie. You're no baby. You're seventeen years old, for Pete's sake."

"But we're planning the Christmas project to-night—"

"Oh, just shut up and get out!"

"Sean . . ."

"*You* don't care about me, either. Just go on and get out. Who needs you anyway?" He gave her a look that would fry eggs on a glacier. "And the *last* thing you need is pizza—fat as *you* are!"

With that, he reached across the front seat, his arm pressing hard against her body as he tugged on the handle. The next thing she knew, he was actually shoving her toward the open door.

To keep from falling, Ruthie swung her feet out onto the ground. But before she could close the door, he revved the engine and backed suddenly. She had to jump away to keep from being struck by the moving car.

Had he really done that? Didn't he care that he might have run over her? *Killed* her even? She couldn't believe it! Sean was supposed to love her! He'd told her enough times.

But he never even looked back. Just spun off, tires squealing, as he tore around the corner and yanked the door closed. All that was left were the car lights fading into the distance—like the glowing red eyes of some monster—and a puff of carbon monoxide trailing from the tail pipe.

Watching the car disappear into the darkness, Ruthie gulped back a sudden rush of tears. A shiver slithered down her spine—not from the cold, but from the eerie feeling that she was not alone. Someone else was out here—behind her. Close. Very close.

A dark-gloved hand grasped her shoulder. In that instant of panic, she froze, the blood in her veins turning to slush. Then the fight-or-flight instinct took over. A rush of adrenaline, like hot lava, gave her the courage to whirl and confront her attacker.

Towering above her was a tall figure in a dark jacket. The face was completely covered by a ski mask. Two sunken holes revealed glistening eyes. A cloud of mist streamed from a slit where a mouth should be. From his throat came the threatening sound of a heavy breather.

The breath Ruthie drew in instinctively returned as a scream that blasted the night like a siren.

"What is it? Whatsa matter?" the figure yelped, both hands on Ruthie's shoulders until she gave him such a push, he hit the pavement on his backside before jerking off his mask.

"Oh!" Ruthie gulped convulsively. "It's only *you*! Stick Gordon, you idiot! You scared me half to death!"

"Well, *you* busted my eardrums." He lumbered to his feet and swiped at the seat of his wet jeans with one gloved hand. "What's wrong with you anyway?"

"You wouldn't have the time to listen." Not that she'd tell this blabbermouth her problems. Scoring points for Shawnee High's basketball team—the Warriors—was not the only thing Stick Gordon excelled in. He also qualified as the class comic. He might just slip up and tell everyone at the youth group meeting that her steady had literally run out on her!

Suddenly, everything seemed to well up inside. Her vision blurred, and hot moisture burned her eyes as a gust of arctic air whipped against them. Blinking away the wetness, Ruthie ducked her head. "Forget it. You just startled me, that's all."

"Sorry." He sprinted ahead, down the outside steps leading to the basement of the church, and waited for her to catch up. With his hand on the door handle, he turned to face her. "Sean giving you a hard time?"

"Whatever made you say a thing like that?" Ruthie asked innocently, stepping up to the door.

"The way he tore out of the parking lot, for one thing. Sorta gave me the idea that all is not perfect in paradise."

Ruthie shrugged. "He had things to do."

"Lovers' spat?"

Lovers? she thought. *Hardly. More like sparring partners for a world-class fight!* "Open the door, Stick. It's freezing out here."

He obliged and stood back to let her pass. Since

when had Stick Gordon read a book on manners? This could only mean that he knew something was wrong and felt sorry for her. Normally, they'd be racing for the door, trying to beat each other through it.

Marching ahead of him as they made their way through the church kitchen and down the hall, Ruthie held her head high and prayed that no one would suspect she'd been crying.

She needn't have worried.

When she stopped near the doorway leading to the fellowship hall, Stick stepped in front of her. "Hold it right there, miss," he ordered. Then, in his usual Keystone-comedy style, he put on his mask again, burst through the door, arms spread wide, and yelled "Boo!"

As all heads swiveled in Stick's direction, he ripped off his mask, to the delight of the younger guys—Stick Gordon look-alikes—who were all sporting their idol's trademark haircut—paintbrush bristles standing straight up on top, closely cropped around the sides.

This time, Ruthie was grateful for the tall guy's goofy antics. In the commotion, she was barely noticed. She quickly slid into a seat on the end, then took a tissue out of her pocket and blew her nose, pretending to be nursing a bad cold.

Taking a quick look around, she saw that the crowd was slim—only about half the regulars. Could be the bitterly cold weather, or maybe the fact that this was Thanksgiving Eve. And of course, she knew where Natalie Ainsworth was. Her best friend, who was also president of the youth group, was in New York City with Cissy Stiles, where Cissy was competing in a

15

model search. That thought only made Ruthie feel more miserable, and she blew her nose again.

Stick made a big production out of moving a chair as close to Amy Ainsworth, Natalie's fifteen-year-old sister, as he could get. Nothing new about that. Nothing new about Amy's reaction, either—flipping her blond hair as she turned her back on him and whispered something to her younger sister Sarah.

After the vice-president opened with a short devotional, Stephanie Kelly stepped to the front. "Okay, we need to discuss our Christmas project—doing something for the single-parent families in town. Right now, we know of about twenty parents and thirty children. We'll have to contact the adults, compile a list of things their kids have asked for, do the shopping and wrapping, deliver gifts and food. . . ."

Ruthie bit her lip as her mind wandered to the Kellys. With Stephanie's eyes shining and her light brown hair pulled back in a ponytail, she could have passed for a high-school senior herself. When the couple had first taken this job—over a year ago—Ruthie had wondered how Steph could have landed a hunk like Andy, with his dark good looks. But it hadn't taken long to discover that Stephanie herself was far from ordinary. She was gentle and kind, and while she usually waited for Andy to take the lead, she balanced out his sometimes overbearing way. She was . . . well, really sweet . . . but everyone respected her. *Too bad I'm not like that*, Ruthie thought with a sigh. *Maybe if I were, I could be more help to Sean. . . .*

It was Stephanie's next question that brought Ruthie back to the meeting. "How do you guys feel about this?"

"Why don't we let the single parents do some of the work themselves?" Stick suggested, eyeing Amy with a look that would melt icicles.

Ruthie didn't feel like arguing with him tonight and was relieved when Amy spoke up. "Come on, Stick. Christmas is a time for giving, or had you forgotten? We're supposed to be *helping* the single parents, not making things *harder* for them."

He shrugged. "Seems to me they'd rather pick out their own stuff—or at least come here and get it rather than have us young people descending on them like a bunch of vultures." He shuffled his big feet. "Some folks might be . . . you know . . . embarrassed about where they live."

No one said a word, which meant the group was mulling it over. Ruthie narrowed her eyes. Stick had never asked any of them over to his house. She'd always wondered why. Now she was getting a clue.

"You're thinking we should give them a Christmas party *here*?" Andy asked.

"Yeah, something like that."

"With a Santa Claus," said Matt, one of the younger guys, who would have seconded any idea presented by his hero.

"Stick would make a great Santa," Philip added.

"Hold it." Stick put up his hands defensively. "That's a job for Andy."

The Kellys looked at each other before Andy continued, "You sure you guys have time for this? Not many made it here tonight, and there's the Christmas cantata coming up. I know several of you are singing in that. Right, Ruthie?"

Ruthie didn't exactly feel a song in her heart right now, but in a weak moment, she *had* agreed to sing a solo for the annual Christmas program. "Oh, most of my evenings are free now," she said in a dull tone. *Ever since Sean started working so much.* Just the thought of him made her feel all goopy inside.

"People usually make time for whatever they want to do," Lana put in sensibly.

Stephanie rose to stand beside Andy. "Right. So let's take a vote."

The decision was unanimous in favor of a party for the children, with each single parent taking home a box of food and other staples afterward.

"I'm not so sure about the Santa Claus part," Andy said with a little frown. "That aspect of Christmas is emphasized too much as it is."

Sarah Ainsworth, looking very serious, spoke up then. Ruthie closed her eyes as the younger girl talked. She could just hear her big sister Natalie saying the same kind of thing. "When we were little, our parents taught us that Santa Claus was just another symbol of the spirit of giving. They explained that God gave His Son as a gift to us, and that's why we give gifts to each other. We never made a big deal over Santa Claus, but we didn't miss out on anything, either."

Amy giggled. "Yeah. Like presents."

There was some laughter and knowing nods.

"So," Stick said, "we could have a Father Christmas or something. Or even a Christmas 'spirit.' Oooohh," he warbled, ghostlike, producing moans from some and snickers from others.

Ruthie cut Stick off with a roll of her eyes and a

suggestion of her own. "Why don't we just have some-one dress up like one of the wise men? We've got those great costumes—complete with beards—for the can-tata. We could use one of those. The wise man could explain what Christmas is all about, and the kids would always remember it."

Stick gaped, bug-eyed. "Awesome!"

While everyone was applauding, Ruthie only felt like crying again. Her best friend was out of town, exploring New York City with her boyfriend and his cousin, and Sean had run off and left her. She might have come up with a great idea . . . for everyone else. But a party was the last thing she cared about right now.

After some discussion about who should be the wise man, Stick was "it."

"Now that that's settled, let's split up into planning groups," Andy said.

"I'll pinch-hit for Natalie," Amy volunteered. "I know she'll want to head up a group when she gets back."

Stick asked to be on Amy's team. Ruthie did, too. As it turned out, with Natalie away, the three of them were the only ones in their group.

Maybe Sean would want to be included. *Maybe.*

"Count Sean in," Ruthie told Amy, hoping and praying that he wouldn't back out—like he had to-night.

Two

"How are you getting home, Ruthie?" Stick asked after the meeting was over.

Amy glanced at Ruthie in surprise, as if realizing for the first time that she'd come alone. Ruthie hadn't wanted to beg a ride when she knew Sean would come back for her. He'd been touchy lately, but he'd always gotten over it.

"Oh, Sean will probably show up any minute now," she said with a show of confidence.

But when everyone in the youth group had left—drifting out of the room in pairs or in clusters—only Ruthie and Stick remained.

"You guys have a way home, I presume," Andy said, walking over to the light switch.

Stick nodded, and Ruthie spoke up quickly, "Sean's picking me up."

Andy glanced at her. "Sorry he didn't make it tonight."

"He had some things to do."

"It's a busy season," Stephanie replied with a wry grin. "Too much to do—too little time. Well, 'night, you two. Stay warm."

Ruthie hurried through the kitchen to the outside door, Stick close behind.

There was no sign of Sean in the parking lot.

"Want to see if you can hitch a ride with the Kellys?"

"I'd rather not," Ruthie admitted, afraid they'd see right through her lame excuses. She'd be apt to blurt out the truth, and they'd come down on Sean. But this was a one-time thing, wasn't it? He'd never pushed her before. And he hadn't really hurt her—at least not physically. She was a big girl now, and she could handle her own problems.

"You can ride with me," Stick offered.

"Terrific!" she said, brightening. *He must be using his grandfather's car.* "Thanks."

"It's right around the corner."

Ruthie hunched her shoulders against the raw wind, punched her fists into the pockets of her parka, and followed Stick. But there was no car parked around the corner. Only his ten-speed bicycle!

"We can't both ride that thing!" she croaked in disbelief.

"Sure we can. You sit on the seat, and I'll stand up and pedal."

"I'll walk. It's only a few blocks."

"No way. You ride, and *I'll* walk."

"Forget it!" she blared, feeling her lips beginning to tremble.

She launched out on her hike, hoping Stick wouldn't see the tears freezing on her face. Oh, great! Some more smudges to join her freckles. Not that every girl could look like Amy Ainsworth or Cissy Stiles.

Stick wheeled his bike along beside her. Suddenly, he stopped and straddled the bar. "I'm not taking no for an answer. Get on!" he ordered.

Too cold to protest, Ruthie hopped onto the seat and clutched the ribbing of his jacket, praying he wouldn't slide on a patch of ice or . . . worse still, that she wouldn't be too *heavy* for him.

Somehow they made it to her street, and before she knew it, Stick was depositing her at her front door.

She slid off the bike, not knowing what to say. "Uh . . . thanks, Stick."

"No big deal. Sorry I can't stay and chew the icicles for a while." As if she wanted him to. "But if you don't mind, I'd like to get home before I freeze to death."

"Sure. And . . . thanks again."

"Any time." He waved, turned his bike around on the icy pavement, and pedaled off into the darkness.

Wonder how far he has to go, she thought—but only for a second—as she opened the front door and rushed inside to thaw out.

In the living room, her little brother, his head full of rusty curls like her own, was sitting cross-legged in front of the TV. "Good program, Justin?" she asked as cheerfully as she could manage.

He glanced around, mumbled something under his breath, then turned to glue his eyes to the screen again. She took that as a definite yes and went to hang up her coat.

In the kitchen, she found her dad sampling freshly baked chocolate chip cookies and her mom sliding another batch into the oven. She sure hoped they'd think her red, watery eyes were caused by the record low temperatures outside. But just in case, she faked a sneeze. Before they could ask about Sean, she jumped right in with a full play-by-play of the youth meeting.

"Great cookies, Mom!" she said, scooping up the last bit of batter in the bowl with one finger and popping it into her mouth. After loading a tray with more of the mouth-watering goodies and milk, she backed out of the kitchen and headed for her room. "See you later. Got some stuff to do for the next meeting."

Safely inside, she set down the tray and closed the door. Then, changing into her flannel pajamas, she put on a tape by a popular Christian artist. But her mind wasn't on the music—nor on the cookies she had wolfed down without tasting.

In fact, staring down at the empty plate, she wondered why she'd done that. She could still see the look of disgust on Sean's face when he'd told her she was getting "fat." *Fat!* If Sean said so, it must be true. Why hadn't she been more careful to stay slim and pretty for him? Maybe *that's* why he hadn't been around much lately. *I'm fat . . . fat . . . fat!*

With a moan, she rushed to the bathroom and stuck her finger down her throat, leaning over the commode to throw up the food she hadn't really wanted. Afterward, feeling weak in the knees, she brushed her teeth, crawled into bed, and turned out the lamp. She lay staring at the ceiling, feeling a warm trickle of tears down her cheeks, pooling in her hair.

"Where are you now that I need you, Nat?" Ruthie whispered into the night. They'd been almost like Siamese twins since their church nursery days. Hardly a day went by that they didn't see each other . . . or talk for hours on the phone, at least. But that was all changing.

Natalie had nabbed one of the best-looking guys in school, Scott Lambert, who'd moved to Garden City from California during his junior year. All the girls had wanted to date the new guy—especially since he drove an awesome red sports car and lived in the ritziest section of town. But Natalie had landed him. And now she was becoming friends with his cousin Cissy Stiles, who was competing in the Dream Teen Model Search this week. Cissy was definitely pretty enough to win. And by the time they came home with stories of their fabulous vacation, Scott and Natalie would be more in love than ever. . . .

But what about me? Ruthie thought with a catch in her throat. *What do I have to tell Natalie? Only that Sean doesn't love me anymore . . . that he insulted me and left me stranded in the cold!*

Oh, but never fear! The damsel in distress was rescued by a not-so-great-looking knight in rusty armor—Stick Gordon and his two-wheeled green machine! Did I ever hit the jackpot!

Rolling over, Ruthie buried her face in the pillow to muffle her wails. But it was hours before she finally fell asleep.

Me? A wise man? Stick thought to himself as he pedaled furiously. *Not if Ruthie Ryan and Sean Jacson have anything to say about it.* Ruthie, the spunkiest girl he'd ever known, was wimping out these days, and Sean, who'd been his friend since their sophomore year, was losing his cool. What was going on with those two?

He pedaled on past Ruthie's neighborhood, toward the outskirts of town, keeping to the side of the road along a wooded area. He made good time, since the country road was pretty well deserted this time of night.

It was slower going, though, when he came to the dirt road on his grandfather's property. They could never afford to have it paved, but he knew every pothole and rut. "I *oughta* know!" he muttered under his breath. "I'm the one who's had to fill 'em with gravel every time it rains!"

The pale moon, shining through the naked branches of the trees, cast eerie shadows on the ground. Stick breathed deeply of the frosty air and exhaled it in a stream of warm mist. The ski mask became damp and stuck to the skin around his mouth. If he didn't get inside soon, it might freeze that way.

Stick thought about this land—four acres, with a small lake on the property—where he'd lived with his mom ever since his dad was killed in a hunting accident. Grandpa had paid it off years ago, but before he could build Grandma the big house she'd always wanted, she'd gotten sick with some kind of slow-growing cancer. It had taken her years to die, and all their money had gone to doctors and medicine. There wasn't any left over to fix up the broken-down shack they were living in.

When Grandma had come home from the hospital the first time, Grandpa had moved into the living room with Stick, where they shared the couch that pulled out into a bed.

Then Grandpa came down with something that made him shake all over. At first, they thought it was just the strain of watching Grandma die by inches. But when Grandpa went to the doctor to see about it, he was told he had Parkinson's disease and that the shakiness and tremors would only get worse.

Stick hadn't minded a bit sharing a bed with Grandpa. In fact, he'd kind of liked the feeling of making sure his grandfather got back in okay when he had to get up in the night.

Then Grandma died, and with the insurance money, his grandfather had bought a double-wide trailer. Stick had finally gotten his own bedroom. Grandpa said he'd even put a little money away for college someday.

He won't have to spend it on me now, Stick thought, rumbling over the little bridge on the last leg toward home. *I'll be going to college on a basketball scholarship.*

A couple of miles down the road, Stick turned into the lane where he lived. Pulling up in front of the trailer, he propped the bicycle against the side and opened the door to the mouth-watering aroma of the turkey his mom had been slow-roasting all afternoon.

"Hi, Grandpa," he said, taking off the ski mask.

His grandfather, who was sitting in a wheelchair, shakily punched a button, turning down the volume on the TV. "Hi, yourshelf." He greeted him with a lopsided smile.

"Turkey smells great, Mom."

Already dressed for work in the uniform she wore as a licensed practical nurse at the hospital, she was holding a hairbrush, which she now aimed in his direction. "Don't you dare touch that bird, young man!"

Stick towered over his mom, but there was no mistaking who was in charge. And although his grandpa's

wheelchair didn't make *him* any less of an authority figure, either, Stick could usually get away with a little
joking around with the old man.

He leaned over and said in a loud whisper, "We'll
raid the kitchen after she's gone."

"You do, and you won't sit down for a week!" Mom
promised, giving her short, dark hair a few swipes with
the brush.

"Okay, Millie." Grandpa tried to wink. "How 'bout
if we eat only the punkin pie?" he drawled in his slow,
slurred speech.

"I'll whip the both of you!" she called over her shoulder, laughing as she disappeared down the hallway.

Stick took off his jacket and threw it on the couch.
Then, after a warning look from his grandfather, he
grabbed up his gear and stashed it in his bedroom.

When he bounded back into the room, his mom was
ready to leave. "You'll never guess who's going to be a
wise man in the Christmas program," he announced.

"Not calling any names"—Grandpa's faded blue
eyes lit up—"but I happen to live . . . with a wise guy."

"Shame on you, Grandpa, talking about Mom that
way."

"Talkin' about a young whippershnap-per," he tried,
but got his tongue tangled up on the last syllables.

"Oh yeah?" Stick growled and reached over to run
his hand through the gray crewcut. He'd cut his grandpa's hair himself. Made it easier to keep it clean.
"Who's the master wisecracker around here?"

Millie shrugged into her coat. "You'll make a good
wise man, Aric," she said affectionately. Neither she
nor Grandpa ever called him by the nickname that had

"stuck" ever since eighth grade, when he'd shot up a good head taller and skinnier than all the other guys. Only in this trailer could he really be himself—Aric Wesley Gordon.

After Mom left, he snagged a stool with the toe of his shoe and dragged it over to the wheelchair. "I don't feel very wise tonight, Grandpa."

"Something . . . wrong?"

"It's Sean. I'm worried about him."

"Hasn't been around much lately."

Stick heaved a sigh. How much should he tell the old man? And what good would it do? All he knew was that Sean Jacson, probably his best friend, was hardly speaking to him anymore. He was putting in a lot of overtime at work and none on the books, so his grades were going down the tube.

Stick decided to give his grandfather the short version. When he was done, his grandfather sat for a long time, staring off into space. Had he been listening? "Grandpa?"

"How's the boy doing . . . with the Lord?"

Stick shook his head. "It's hard to tell. He was coming along, but lately he's been pulling away from the crowd at church. And since he's been working nights, I haven't seen him except in class. I guess . . . we've failed him, Grandpa."

Even with his muscles so weak that he slumped forward in his chair, the real Grandpa was as strong as ever, Stick thought. And when the old man looked at Stick with that steady gaze, his meaning was clear.

Intercepting the thought, Stick nodded. *The Golden Rule.* That was Grandpa's motto: "Do to others what you'd want them to do to you." Suddenly, seeing his grandfather's pitiful, twisted body, Stick had to fight back the tears. If his grandpa could sit in that wheelchair day after day without complaining, Stick could work out—hard—at basketball practice, or pedal that bicycle wherever he had to go, and not grumble about his sore muscles. At least he was young and healthy.

He reached out in a clumsy attempt to pat the old man's hand. Grandpa held on—his grip surprisingly firm—closed his eyes, and began to pray. The garbled words that came out were not much better than a bunch of sounds a little kid makes when he's learning to talk. But Stick got the point. So did God, he figured.

Later, when Stick called Sean's house, Mrs. Jacson answered. "He's not home yet," she said. "He took Ruthie to church. Didn't you go?"

"Yes, ma'am. Just thought he might be home by now."

She sighed. "Well, you know Sean. I guess he's still with Ruthie. I'll tell him you called."

Stick hung up, wondering where his friend could be. He *wasn't* with Ruthie, that was for sure.

"I'll try again in the morning," he told his grandpa while he was getting him ready for bed.

Later in his own room, with Grandpa down for the night, Stick remembered the old man's keen-eyed look and the slurred prayer that had followed, and he added a P. S.: "Lord, help me figure out what *I'd* want Sean to do for *me* if the shoe were on the other foot."

Three

Ruthie cracked an eyelid and stretched, feeling about as energetic as a slug on a cold sidewalk. Speaking of sidewalks . . . that's where Natalie would be right about now—somewhere on the sidewalks of New York City, cheering Cissy on! Cissy Stiles was supposed to ride on a float in Macy's Thanksgiving Day Parade, Ruthie remembered. If she was lucky, she might just get to see her best friend *and* Cissy—everyone's arch rival and the prettiest girl at Shawnee High until she'd graduated last spring.

On the other hand, the idea was far from comforting. Maybe breakfast would put things into perspective.

Ruthie dragged herself out of bed, shuffled into the bathroom, and splashed a little cold water on her face. Somewhat revived, she moved slowly toward the living room. Justin had gotten there ahead of her and was up to his eyeballs in a cartoon.

"Aren't you going to watch the parade?"

"Later." He gave her a mischievous look and grabbed for the control. "I wanna see how this comes out first."

"We might see Natalie and Cissy."

He shrugged. "I know what they look like."

Any other morning, she would have pounced on him, called him a "little monster," and wrestled him for the remote. Today, she just didn't feel like it.

When she passed him on her way to the kitchen, he pouted. "You're no fun anymore."

"I'm not a seven-year-old kid, Justin," she snapped, and Sean's words echoed in her brain. *You're no baby, Ruthie. You're seventeen years old!* Sean hadn't meant that as a compliment.

In the kitchen, she put a couple of cinnamon buns on a paper plate while her mother struggled with the giblets stuck in the turkey's carcass. "I think they pack these things in cement!" she grumbled.

Ruthie set the microwave for twenty-nine seconds. "After I eat a little something, I'll help . . . if you want me to."

Mom was blown away by the offer, judging from the look of total shock on her face. When she found her voice, she asked about Sean. "Will he be eating with us?"

"I don't know," Ruthie hedged, ducking her head into the refrigerator, looking for milk to add to the chocolate syrup she'd spooned into a mug. "He . . . wasn't sure last night what his mom's plans were. He'll probably call."

"Well, there's plenty," her mother said. "Ah!" Dislodging the giblets at last, she plopped them into a pot.

Ruthie nuked her hot chocolate, then went to her room, where she could eat unobserved. She sat, staring at the tray. Why couldn't she have settled for a small bowl of cereal? No wonder she looked like a pig!

Resisting the temptation to take a single bite, she

rushed to the bathroom and flushed the food, then changed into her jeans. They seemed looser already. Still, she could pinch at least half an inch of fat.

She was eyeing herself in her dresser mirror when the phone rang, and her heart jumped. "Cool it," she told her reflection. "Wouldn't want anyone to get the idea you're anxious or anything."

"It's for you, Ruthie," her mother called from the kitchen.

Ruthie raced in, then drew a deep breath and forced herself to sound casual when she picked up. "Hello?"

"Hi, Ruthie. It's Stick."

"Oh." What a drag. Unfortunately, Stick probably got the message, too, but she couldn't disguise her disappointment.

"I've been trying to reach Sean. Thought he might be with you."

"No, he's not here," she said, realizing that this was the first time in almost two years she hadn't known Sean's whereabouts.

"I'm worried about him, Ruthie."

"Because of what happened last night?"

"Oh, not just that. Things have been weird with him for a long time. I guess I sort of ignored it."

She knew the feeling. "It's a hard time for him, Stick. You know. All that stuff with his family."

Stick let out a long breath. "Yeah. He needs friends now more than ever . . . and God."

Ruthie's mouth dropped open. Look who was talking! Stick Gordon—the class comic. Maybe he *did* have a serious thought in his head once in a while.

Finally, breaking the silence, Stick wound up the

conversation. "Well, if you see him, tell him I'm trying to get in touch."

If. Even *Stick* had his doubts. "Sure. 'Bye." She hung up without getting into it.

With her mom busy basting the turkey, Ruthie escaped to her room again before any questions could be asked. The strain was killing her. And there was no one to talk to.

Grabbing a little diary she'd gotten for her birthday, she propped herself up in bed, letting her mind wander back to the good old days—her sophomore year at Shawnee High. She'd never really noticed Sean until Stick brought him to a youth meeting. By the end of the year, they were pairing off to talk when the crowd got together. But their first real date wasn't until their junior year, when Sean got his old clunker.

It was wintertime. The heater hadn't worked even back then, and she'd almost frozen. But when he put his arms around her at the front door and his lips touched hers, she didn't think she'd ever be cold again!

She loved him, and now she realized that she'd let him down. Stick was right. Sean needed friends who could steer him to the only Source of help.

Ruthie stared, unblinking, for so long her eyes felt hot and dry. Since she couldn't call Natalie, she decided to write down all her thoughts and feelings. Maybe something would click—something that would explain why Sean didn't hang around as much as he used to. With her left hand, she reached for the tiny little roll around her middle. Was she really that fat?

Natalie hadn't said anything. But then, Natalie was . . . well, Nat. She liked *everyone.*

"Ruthie?"

Hearing a small voice from the doorway, she looked up from her book. "Come on in, Justin."

Strange, how much smaller and younger he seemed. His freckles looked like mud spatters on his pale skin, and his curls tumbled like rusty wires around his little-boy face.

"You can watch the parade now," he said.

"Oh, is your cartoon over?"

"Nope. It's not too good. The parade is better."

"Well, thanks, little bro."

He turned away, but not before she noticed the hang-dog look in his brown eyes—like a cocker spaniel who'd been scolded for making a puddle on the living room carpet. Were her doldrums rubbing off on him?

I don't care if it is over a month before New Year's, she thought with a sudden burst of determination. *I'm turning over a new leaf.*

"Mom!" she called, rushing into the kitchen. "Have I got a challenge for you!" She held out her mass of coppery curls on both sides. "Think you could cut a path through this jungle?"

With a towel wrapped around her freshly shampooed hair, Ruthie spread a sheet on the living room floor and set a chair on it. Unaware that life was about to change drastically, her dad merely glanced up, lifted his eyebrows, and continued browsing through the new car ads in a current issue of *Time* magazine.

On the floor behind him, Justin was playing with his rubber snakes, pretending to be wallowing in a pit with a thirty-foot python. She wished it would hurry and swallow him.

"Parade's starting," Ruthie announced, sitting down in the chair.

"Okay," her mom called from the kitchen. "Be right there just as soon as I've finished basting the bird."

She was back in a second, wielding her scissors. "You're *sure* about this?"

Ruthie took a deep breath. On television, the parade commentator was saying that a turkey is so stupid it will hold its head up and stare into the rain until it drowns. Well, she didn't plan to be stupid where Sean was concerned. *I'm going to take the plunge. Do something different. Now is the time to make some changes.*

"There's the look I want." She pointed to one of her mother's trade magazines—*Stylish Hairdos*. "You can do that cut, can't you?"

"We-ll, I haven't been a beautician all that long, you know. But I think I can handle it."

Ruthie made a face and screwed up her courage. "Go for it!"

As her mom removed the towel that was draped around her head, Ruthie kept her gaze fastened on the television screen. Macy's famous Thanksgiving Day Parade was beginning, and the crowd went wild. Bands marched and flags flew. Elaborate floats glided by on invisible wheels.

In the middle of everything, Ruthie heard *snip, snip, snip.* She was afraid to move her head, but in her peripheral vision, she kept track of the rust-colored curls falling like confetti. They lay like oodles of tomato-noodles all over the sheet.

"This is pretty exciting," her mom said.

"What's exciting? The parade . . . or scalping me?"

"Both, actually. But I was just thinking—I've never known anyone in the parade or, for that matter, anyone who was in New York City, *watching* the parade." She gestured toward the TV with her scissors. "Is that Scott and Natalie?" she asked as the camera panned the cheering crowd.

They couldn't be sure. But they recognized Cissy, riding on the pink-flowered Top Ten Modeling Agency float with nine other girls who were in the competition. Three of them would be contracted by the agency, Natalie had told Ruthie.

Snip, snip, snip.

Cissy's hair is short, Ruthie consoled herself, then had to add truthfully, *Yeah, but she has a beautiful face to go with it, not to mention a flawless complexion. With my freckles, I look like I have a face full of zits!*

"Why is Cissy wearing sunglasses?" Ruthie's mom asked. "None of the other models are wearing them."

"Maybe she just wants to be a cool dude," Justin piped up.

Dad peered over his glasses. "Or maybe it's a technique to attract the judges' attention. It sure got ours."

"Well, she doesn't need anything else with that perfect face and that toned figure." Maureen Ryan reached for a bottle of mousse. "Great hair, too."

Cissy, in a white faux fur coat, was waving to the crowds of people thronging the streets and hanging out of the windows of tall buildings. She looked spectacular, Ruthie decided—with her cornsilk-blond hair swishing around her face. In those shades, she could pass for a celebrity. "She's bound to win in that getup."

Ruthie remembered when Cissy had seemed to live in another world—a really different world from hers and Natalie's. But that was before the tornado had turned all their worlds upside down. It was Natalie and her Christian witness that night that had changed Cissy's life. And now they were probably better friends than ever, Ruthie thought with more than a twinge of envy.

For the umpteenth time, her thoughts shifted to Sean. *I haven't done much to change Sean's life—for the better anyway.*

Cissy's float moved out of sight and several others rolled into view. Then came a marching band, preceded by high-stepping Rockettes in swallow-tailed tuxedo jackets and shorts.

"I'll bet they're freezing in those skimpy things," Mom said, then put down her scissors and began to brush, blow dry, crunch, and pick. The thought occurred to Ruthie that she might just float away—like some of those huge helium-filled balloons in the parade. She felt tons lighter.

When she was done, her mom carefully removed the towel, tugged Ruthie to her feet, and twirled her around. "Ta-da! What do you think, Grady?"

But before he could answer, Justin crawled over to the spot where some of Ruthie's hair had fallen on the carpet and shrieked, "Worms, worms! We've been invaded!"

He grabbed for the blow dryer, but his mom reached it before he could turn it on. "You'll have this stuff all over the house," she scolded.

Dad looked like he might cry. "Where's my little girl gone?"

"Under the worms," Justin informed him.

But her dad ignored the comment. "I like it," he nodded, looking thoughtful.

It wasn't exactly a rave review, but after all, a different hairstyle could hardly compete with a new Infiniti or even Macy's Thanksgiving Day Parade. "What do *you* think, Mom?" Ruthie really wanted to know.

"You're gorgeous, hon. You look so grown-up, and the cut brings out your beautiful eyes."

Oh, great! Then it would "bring out" her freckles, too! Besides, what kind of unbiased critique would you expect from your own mother—especially if she also happened to be your hair stylist?

"Why don't you go look for yourself?"

Ruthie trekked into the bathroom, scrunched her eyes shut, then opened them and peered into the mirror.

Her first impression was of a neat upsweep—lots of volume on top, with the hair feathered toward her forehead. Wisps curled at her temples, and several longer tendrils swirled lightly in front of her ears.

She picked up a hand mirror to take a look at the back. Here the curls were gradually tapered to a soft wave that fanned across the back of her neck.

Hand trembling, Ruthie laid the mirror down and studied her face. So much of it was showing—not round anymore, but an oval. Her brown eyes looked huge, and she hardly noticed her freckles at all.

"Ruthie Ryan," she spoke into the mirror, "if that's really *you* in there . . . you look fantastic!"

Feeling better than she'd felt in days, Ruthie spent

the rest of the morning and part of the afternoon helping her mom in the kitchen. By dinnertime, she was ready to eat a cow! Well, after her mom had cooked all day, she certainly couldn't insult her by eating like a bird, could she?

When Sean didn't show up for dinner, Ruthie took second helpings of everything, topping it all off with pumpkin pie and a huge dollop of whipped cream.

For a while, the fabulous meal comforted her. But when her dad asked about Sean, she felt the tears threatening. She excused herself from the table, went to the bathroom, and repeated the purging procedure of the night before. The hot bile stung her throat, but it was worth it. When she patted her stomach, it definitely felt flatter. Of course, she didn't plan to do this too often. She wasn't stupid. But this was Thanksgiving—no day to start a diet.

Later, while the whole family was watching the football game, she felt another surge of self-pity. Last year, Sean had eaten dinner with them and watched a game on TV. Maybe she'd been wrong to say she'd go steady at this age. It felt so lonely when he wasn't with her.

Then Natalie called from New York. "I'll give you the details later," she promised, all breathless, "but I just had to tell you about our day. Did you see us on TV?"

"We saw Cissy—" Ruthie began, feeling she hardly knew this person who sounded so different somehow. "But we weren't sure we spotted you and Scott."

"Well," Natalie went on in a giddy tone, "would you believe that we ran into this homeless woman living in a cardboard box in an *alley*, and Scott invited her to eat Thanksgiving dinner with us in this elegant restaurant. Oh, it was *awesome*! And the hotel is *fabulous*!"

Awesome? Fabulous? The old Natalie never resorted to teen clichés. Then came the clincher. "Scott took me up to the forty-eighth floor—to a revolving restaurant called The View. And what a view! New York City at night! Ruthie, it was so romantic! And tomorrow night's the finals of the modeling competition. Oh, and Cissy got a black eye when a guy with a camcorder backed out of a room into the hallway. . . . But here comes Scott. I'll have to tell you later."

Just when Ruthie figured Natalie was about to hang up, she got quiet. "But, Ruthie, how are things with *you*?"

Good ol' Nat. Always thinking about the other person. The world could be coming to an end, but Natalie Ainsworth would be there . . . caring. Ruthie was almost jealous of *that*.

"Oh, great!" she forced herself to say. "The usual, you know."

Ruthie felt even lonelier after talking with Natalie. Cissy would probably become a famous model. Natalie and Scott would go steady after this trip. And Ruthie? Well, she was losing ground. No exciting trips planned. No career. No boyfriend—at least not for long. All she had to look forward to was a P.E. major at the local junior college and coaching young girls in sports. Whewee.

Feeling her empty stomach pushing against her backbone, she fixed herself half a turkey sandwich and washed it down with diet soda. So why was her stomach still growling? *Get over it*, she rumbled back.

She turned in early and made herself say her

prayers—this was Thanksgiving, after all, and it seemed the right thing to do. She tried counting her blessings, but they fizzled out when she came to "Sean." Could she still count *him*?

~~~~~~~

Stick tried all day to reach Sean. But the guy either hadn't gotten his messages, or he just didn't want to return his calls.

Since his mom didn't have to work tonight, Grandpa had insisted he take the car—and go look for Sean. Good thing, Stick thought. He'd never have made it to the end of the long dirt road on his bike, the way that icy wind was howling, slinging chunks of ice and snow into the windshield.

He drove by Ruthie's house, but Sean's car wasn't there. It wasn't parked in front of Sean's house, either. Unless his schedule had changed, his friend still had Wednesday and Thursday nights off of work. Maybe he was at his dad's new apartment. Stick had no idea where that was.

He did remember that all kinds of stuff was going on at church, though. With the cantata coming up, maybe Ruthie had a rehearsal or something. Taking a chance that Sean would be with her, Stick drove by the church. But he didn't see any sign of a beat-up green Chevy.

He passed the town's only theater, but he didn't spot Sean in the long line outside. Besides, if Sean had decided to take in a flick, wouldn't he have called his old buddy Stick to go with him? The only other guys Sean hung out with were their mutual friends at church or school. And they always did stuff together. Still, he doubted they'd be planning anything. Thanksgiving was family time.

He drove through town, then cut down a side street toward the Pizza Palace. Yes! One of the two cars in the back parking lot was Sean's.

Stick pulled to a stop and hurried in out of the cold. It felt good in here. But what was that smell? Above the tangy, spicy aroma of pizza sauce was a musty odor. Smoke. Someone was smoking. Nonsmokers could sniff it out every time.

Probably hearing the door slam, a girl looked up from cleaning the front counter, her dark ponytail swishing like a puppy dog's tail. Stick recognized Phyllis Haney, who'd worked here even before she graduated last year.

"Five turkey pizzas to go," Stick quipped. "Oh, and hold the cranberries."

"You turkey!" She laughed. "But you're a little late. We're closing early tonight."

"Guess I'll just have to go gobble with my buddy over there."

Phyllis glanced over toward a booth in the back, where Sean was sitting with a couple of guys Stick didn't know. From the way she lit up—like a sparkler on the Fourth of July—one of them must be her boyfriend.

When Stick walked over and spoke, the two guys seemed friendly enough. One of them—a guy who looked to be in his early twenties, old enough to grow a thin mustache—was the smoker. Since Sean didn't introduce them, the stranger did the honors himself and stuck out his hand. "Hi. I'm Cliff."

"Oh, and this is Bud," Sean put in before Stick

could say anything. "Phyllis's brother. They work at the warehouse." His next words held a ring of sarcasm. "Stick Gordon here's the school's star basketball player. You guys have probably heard of him."

The one who'd introduced himself as Cliff squinted through the smoke. "Gordon. Yeah, I've heard you're a cinch to make it to the pros."

"Here's hoping," Stick said, wondering why Sean was glaring at him like that. "Hey, Sean, you wanna go for a spin?"

"On your *bike*?" he snorted.

Stick felt himself shrink a couple of feet. "I've got the car tonight."

"Not now, buddy." Sean's tough-guy expression softened a little. "We've . . . uh . . . I've already made other plans."

"Okay, see you around." Stick lifted his hand, pivoted toward the door, and almost ran into Phyllis. She had her coat on and had fixed herself up. Lipstick. Eye makeup. The works. She sure had a thing for one of those guys.

She stepped around Stick and walked back to the booth with a drop-dead smile, saying in a sing-songy voice, "I'm ready."

Stick moved on through the door. *There are two cars outside. Who's going where?*

"Be right with you," Sean said and headed for the rest room, planning to make sure Stick was long gone before he returned. Not that he was doing anything wrong, but it could look that way if someone wanted to make something of it. It's just that he'd never done anything like this before. On the other hand, Phyllis *had* . . . or so it had been rumored around town.

Bud and Cliff had already left by the time Sean was back. Phyllis was waiting for him by the back door. She motioned him out, then switched off the light and locked up.

Sean glanced around before reminding himself he shouldn't worry about being seen. Stick had left. It was past Ruthie's curfew. And the one who would be on his case the most—Miss High-and-Mighty Natalie Ainsworth—was in New York with her high-class boyfriend. *Man, if I had a car like Scott's!*

But he didn't. He had a rattletrap that even his dad, the overhaul genius, could barely keep running. He wasn't about to ask *him* for anything anyway. A lot his dad cared—about him *or* his mother. Otherwise, he wouldn't be blaming her for his own mistakes.

Sean welcomed the blast of cold air that struck his face before he helped Phyllis in and walked around the car to get in on the driver's side. Thanksgiving. Right. At the youth group, he'd heard plenty about counting your blessings. But what did *they* know? He'd count 'em . . . if he had any.

A twinge of guilt pricked his conscience. At least he had a car. On the days Phyllis didn't drive her mom's car to work, she had to wait for Bud to pick her up. Still, it wasn't as bad for a *girl* not to have wheels. You could bet Phyllis's *boyfriend* would have some.

He slid in behind the steering wheel, started the engine, and looked over at her. He hadn't noticed before, but she was kind of pretty, with her hair down like that.

"I'm not going to make a habit out of this," Sean

told her as the car chugged out onto the main road.

She smiled and shrugged her shoulders. "Up to you."

"I figure," he began, a little nervous now that they were really going through with this, "a few bucks here and there won't make that much difference."

"Exactly."

Not wanting to sound like some kind of dork, he tried to make polite conversation. "Got a boyfriend, Phyllis?"

"Did you know Greg Tompkins?"

"Sure. He graduated last year."

"Well, the day he went off to college, he told me he'd love me forever. But I found out later he had a new girlfriend the very first week, the creep."

When she started talking about Stick and his chances of making it big in basketball, Sean felt a sinking in his gut. Some guys had all the luck. He was glad for Stick, of course, but he couldn't help wondering, *When's it going to be my turn?*

Driving up in front of Phyllis's house, he put thoughts of Stick and his bright future behind him. Sean had more in common with Phyllis anyway; she lived with only one parent, too. A lot of kids lived like that.

Phyllis wasn't a kid though. She was a grown woman now—over eighteen and a high school graduate. She could do anything she wanted.

Sean kept the engine idling while Phyllis opened her purse.

Then he reached into his pocket and pulled out a small wad of bills.

Four

The day after Thanksgiving, Ruthie figured her mom would want to hit the malls first thing, since yesterday's paper had been full of ads for the pre-Christmas sales.

Ruthie, on the other hand, had planned to stay home—in case Sean called. "But why don't you and Dad go, Mom? I'll take care of Mons—Justin," she corrected herself just in the nick of time. No matter how appropriate the old nickname might be, she'd decided never again to purposely say anything that could hurt another person. Not anymore, now that she knew how it felt. "Oh, and could we put up the Christmas tree?" she added.

"This early?" Dad slanted her a questioning look.

"Whee! Whee! The Christmas tree!" Justin chanted, doing a good imitation of a jack-in-the-box. "Me and Ruthie can decorate it, and you two can buy me a whole bunch of presents to put under it."

"You'll get a sack of coal, if you're not careful," their dad teased, tousling Justin's mop of curls.

Ruthie knew how much her mother always dreaded tackling the artificial tree with all those little slots for the branches. She usually ended up scratching her arms or picking her sweater. Right now, though, Mom was grinning. "Well, that *would* be a load off my mind."

Dad wasn't impressed. "The biggest sale day of the year—and you two expect me to brave a bunch of bargain-hungry women?"

"Now, honey, you know you've been wanting to look at new cars." She winked at Ruthie. "Why don't you do that, then meet me for lunch? Do us good to get out for a change—just the two of us—don't you think?"

He squinted, studying her for a minute. Mom did look pretty, Ruthie thought—sort of young and flushed. "Guess it wouldn't hurt."

So Dad had backed down—even after putting up an argument in the beginning. *Maybe that's the way men operate*, Ruthie thought, then moaned inwardly, *Maybe it's not Sean, after all. Maybe it's me. I'm just too sensitive. He probably didn't mean anything by what he said. And if I don't get upset with him, then maybe he won't get upset with me . . . if he ever comes around again, that is.*

To her relief, Sean called after her folks left, and asked to see her right away. Was he kidding? She'd only been waiting forty-one hours and thirty-two minutes for this call!

Still, when she took a look around, she wondered if she'd lost her mind, saying he could come over. Everything was a mess. Christmas tree parts spread out from one end of the living room to the other. Justin, rummaging in the ornament boxes. . . .

As for herself, yikes! She dashed to her bedroom and looked in the mirror. Her hair still looked great, thank goodness, but she ought to do something about those dark circles under her eyes. Concealer would help, she hoped as she applied the cover stick, then a dab of lip gloss. She just wished her sloppy, old T-shirt would cover her fat.

It felt weird a little later, when Sean was standing in the middle of the living room, surrounded by the artificial greenery. Ruthie—who'd never met a stranger in her life—was suddenly completely tongue-tied. And this was her steady—the guy she loved!

"Sorry I didn't call yesterday," he said. "Mom and I spent the day with her parents in Cairo."

"It's okay." He didn't owe her any explanations, she supposed. It was just that before, he'd always volunteered to tell her where he was and what he was doing when he wasn't with her.

She gave him the once-over. He looked terrific. When he'd first gotten his job at the warehouse, he'd told her that all the lifting, stretching, loading, and working the levers on the carts were great muscle-builders. "Better than a workout at a health club." Well, he was right.

"You got your hair cut," he said, breaking the awkward silence.

He'd noticed then. "Yeah. Mom did it."

"Turn around."

She spun around for him.

"Looks like a picture in a magazine."

"That's where I got the idea." She took a deep breath before facing him again.

"Looks good on you."

She met his eyes for an instant. His reaction was about as enthusiastic as her dad's had been. But this wasn't the time for compliments. Not when there were more important things at stake—like their whole future.

Sean smiled a little and looked away. "Hey, Monster, how's it going?"

Justin glanced up from the box he was plowing through and grinned, then held up a shiny red glass ball. He hadn't seemed to notice that Sean had called him a less-than-complimentary name. "Betcha don't know what Disney character is named for outer space."

"Snow White," Sean guessed.

Justin threw back his head and laughed, then said in a superior tone, "Nope! Pluto. Got another one. What baseball player is named after a tree?"

Sean shrugged. "Beats me."

"Baby root," Justin said. "You know, Babe Ruth?"

"Everyone knows Babe Ruth."

Sean lunged for Justin, who fell over and rolled away, taunting, "You didn't say it 'cause you didn't know it."

By this time, Sean had pinned Justin in a hammer lock and was tickling him while he howled for mercy. And before long, the little glass ball lay broken under their churning feet.

"Look what you guys did!" Ruthie scolded.

"Oh no!" Justin moaned theatrically. "It was Mom's favorite. Her great-great-great-grandmother gave it to her."

"Oh, she did not, silly. Mom bought those red ones at an after-Christmas sale last year at the drug store." Ruthie looked toward the ceiling, shaking her head.

Sean gave Justin one final tickle. "Let's get this mess cleaned up." He glanced at Ruthie as he reached over to pick up the pieces. "Want me to put the tree together?"

"That would be super." She was grateful for more than the offer. She was actually glad the little red ball had gotten smashed; it had also broken the ice, and she felt herself melting. "Tie him up if you have to," she told Sean with a sassy cock of her head. "I've got to go wash the breakfast dishes."

It wasn't long before Sean came in with the shards of glass. He threw the pieces into the trash can, then scooped up a stack of dirty dishes and brought them over to the sink, where Ruthie was swishing detergent through the warm water. "Justin's cleaning his room," he told her.

"How in the world did you manage that?"

He moved in close, nudging her shoulder with his. "I promised we'd decorate the tree when he finished, and then maybe the three of us could go to McDonald's for lunch. Hey—" he turned her around to face him—"I'm sorry for the way I acted the other night. I've been too ashamed to even call. But I love you, and you're my girl." He leaned his forehead against hers. "You *are* still my girl . . . aren't you?"

How could she stay mad at him when he was looking at her like that? Besides, was what Sean had done really so unforgivable? He'd only let her out at the church, and that *was* where she was going, wasn't it? She thought of the Bible passage where Jesus taught that people should forgive each other—not seven times, but "seventy times seven." If she remembered that lesson right, she hadn't even gotten *started* on this forgiveness thing.

She nestled close. "Sure, Sean, sure I am," she whispered, feeling him relax. "I guess I'm not always so easy to get along with, either."

"You're my girl," he repeated, "and I love you."

He kissed the tip of her nose, then her lips, sweetly, softly. "You love me, too, don't you, Ruthie?"

Didn't he know? She'd loved him since their sophomore year. It had felt so special to have a steady boyfriend. She always had a date. They were an item. She nodded, looking up at him through her eyelashes.

"Then *tell* me."

She ignored the edge in his voice. "I love you, Sean."

Their lips touched again, but at a gagging sound from behind, they sprang apart. It was only Justin, crossing his eyes as he choked himself.

"You little monster!" Sean yelled and ran into the living room after him.

Noticing that the hot water was running over into the other side of the sink, Ruthie turned off the faucet and wiped the steam off the window. *Of course I love him. Who wouldn't? So we had a little misunderstanding. It was only . . . temporary.*

At McDonald's, Ruthie wasn't sure what to order. "I might just have a salad," she told Sean.

He looked at her like she'd just grown another head. "You *hate* salads."

She made a face at him. He knew her too well. Anyway, she probably couldn't force down all that green stuff without dressing, and she'd read that a couple of tablespoonfuls could contain more calories than a full-course meal. On the other hand, a hamburger and fries spelled f-a-t! *F-a-t!*

"Let's just take something home. We still have

some decorating to do. Maybe we can get it done before Mom and Dad get home."

Justin was all for that idea. "I bet they'll have lots of presents for me!"

Back home, while they ate their lunch in the breakfast room, Ruthie could almost feel the fat grams collecting around her waist. She decided to eat little bites and chew for a long time.

Sean and Justin polished off their meals long before she was through, and she took advantage of the privacy to dump her half-eaten burger in the trash can.

A little later, Sean brought in another broken ornament. "What's this?" he asked, spotting the remains of her lunch.

"I couldn't eat it all," she said guiltily.

"Why did you order it then?"

"Well, I *told* you I only wanted a salad . . . and you made fun of me." She hoped she didn't sound like she was whining.

"So? You can eat what you want to. But that's like throwing away my hard-earned money, babe."

She sniffed and shrugged her shoulders. "Big deal. I'll pay you back for my lunch if it'll make you feel any better."

His ears turned red, and she didn't like the looks of that scowl. "*Money* isn't the problem, Ruthie." From the way he said that, she knew she'd stepped on a sensitive issue. "What bugs me is the way you always have a comeback for everything I say, and I'm getting sick and tired of it!" By this time, he was shouting.

Justin whirled in just then like a miniature tornado. "Don't you yell at my sister!" he yelled.

For a minute, Ruthie was afraid Sean was going to turn on Justin, but he only grinned. "Aw, I was just kidding around, buddy." He made a sudden move. "It's really *you* I'm after!"

With that, he tore out after her little brother, wrestled him to the floor in the other room, and began to tickle him as Justin screamed for mercy.

Even though she hadn't eaten much lunch, Ruthie suddenly felt like a ton of bricks had just descended on her. Why was it she was always saying or doing the wrong thing around Sean? He was right about something else, too. How could she throw away food when people were starving in Africa . . . and India . . . and Bosnia. . . ?

What was happening to the two of them anyway? And how awful that a little kid felt he had to defend her. It was humiliating.

Shaking off her gloom, Ruthie dried her hands and joined Sean and Justin in the living room, where they'd settled their tickling match.

No one said much while they finished decorating the tree. But when they turned on the lights, the heavy mood lifted.

"Awesome!" Justin said, his eyes shining, reflecting the multicolored bulbs.

There *were* some vacant spots, Ruthie noticed, and a few patches where the ornaments were hung too close together. But Mom always rearranged them anyway.

When Sean was ready to leave, he put his hands on her shoulders and pulled her close. "Everything okay now?"

"Sure," she said, lifting her face for him to touch

his lips to hers. "Everything's cool."

But everything's not cool between Sean and me, Ruthie wrote in her diary the following Sunday night, after driving herself home from a youth group meeting in her mom's car.

I'm not sure what's wrong. Maybe I'm too possessive or something. But Sean hasn't been around lately, and he didn't show up for church this morning—or youth group tonight. It's embarrassing when the kids at church ask me where he is, and I hate to admit I don't have a clue.

Oh, I know he's busy. He's been working a lot lately, but he doesn't have the Sunday-night shift. Maybe he had to help his mom, or work on the car. Or maybe he's studying for midterms. At least, that's what I've been telling everyone.

The truth is, though, he's never studied much. So I've been coming pretty close to telling a lie. . . .

Ruthie put her pen down and fingered the silver chain around her neck, feeling for the little white dove with the rhinestone for an eye. Like some of the others in the youth group, she wore it all the time as a reminder that God's Spirit was with her. Right now, she needed that reminder. She picked up her pen again and began to write:

My relationship with Sean is not as much fun as it used to be. So maybe this is a test of our feelings for each other. I really don't want to be just a "fair-weather" friend to him. I want to be the kind of friend Stick was talking about. . . .

A prayer began to form in her mind, and she scribbled furiously: *Lord, I know Sean is not taking his problems to you and trusting you to help him out. I'm not sure*

he knows how. He wasn't at youth group when Stephanie
was teaching us how to put on "the whole armor of God,"
like it says in Ephesians, and fight against Satan when he
attacks us with his fiery darts. Weird. It just came to me
that maybe Sean doesn't know you at all.

It's scary to think that—if he drops out of youth group
completely—I might be the only Christian left in his life!

At the thought, she felt a little chill, then realized
Justin had opened the door and burst into her room.
"Writin' secrets about your boyfriend?"

Ruthie snapped the diary shut and slid it under a pillow. "It's really none of your business. But I happened
to be writing a prayer." At the funny look on his face,
she hurried on. "Did you come in to say good-night?"

"Nope. I came to tell you the phone's for you."

Ruthie jumped to her feet. "Then why didn't you
tell me?"

"I just did."

Ruthie groaned and stepped around him in a mad
dash for the kitchen. Maybe God was already answering her prayer.

———

Ruthie returned to her room, still stunned that Mom
and Dad had agreed to a school-night movie date with
Sean tomorrow night, who had swapped shifts with a co-
worker in order to get the night off. To her shock, she
found her brother sitting in the middle of her bed, reading her diary. "Justin! What do you think you're doing?"

He flinched as if she'd hit her. "I didn't think you'd
care. You said it was just a prayer."

Ruthie was ready to jerk the book away from him

and wallop him with it when something in his expression stopped her. He reminded her of herself when Sean yelled at her. But Justin was just a little boy.

Taking a deep breath, she sat down on the bed beside him. "You were reading the prayer, huh?" she asked, still not sure whether to believe him or not.

He nodded. "Yeah. I always say the same things—like 'Thank you for the food' and 'God bless everybody.' I wanted to see what *you* say."

"So . . . what do you think?"

He ducked his head and looked up at her with an angelic smile. "Well . . . I couldn't read all the words, and some of it looked like chicken-scratching."

"Oh, you!" She grabbed the diary and shoved him back on her pillows. He chortled with glee, but Ruthie was dead serious when she said, "Really, Justin, a diary is very personal. You have no business sneaking around reading something someone else wrote without that person's permission."

"Is it okay if I read your diary?"

"No, it is *not* okay!" She gave him a playful shove. "Now scoot. Isn't it nearly your bedtime?"

"Not till Mom tells me for the hundredth time."

Ruthie grinned. She knew how to get rid of him. "You look so cute I think I'm going to kiss you." She made a move toward him.

Justin let out a howl, jumped off the bed, and lickety-split, he was gone. Now all she had to do was get rid of her lingering doubts about Sean.

Five

It was like old times the next night at the theater. Sean dug into the popcorn, not seeming to notice that Ruthie wasn't eating much of it. He laughed at the jokes, got really into the action scenes, and held her hand at the end when the guy got the girl. Ruthie felt herself relax and enjoy the moment. He hadn't even complained when she told him about the eleven o'clock curfew.

Yeah, just like old times! she thought as he pulled up into her driveway.

He switched off the ignition, then turned in his seat, draping one arm over the steering wheel. "I don't know when we can go out again, Ruthie," he said in a dull tone.

"Why not?" Maybe he was going to tell her it was over. And just when she was beginning to think everything was going to work out.

"I have to read three books and write that paper for English class by the end of next week. . . ." He looked over at her with a grin that would melt a glacier. "You wouldn't want to help me out, would you?"

"Help you . . . how?"

"Well, you've probably read the books. You could just give me the highlights . . . you know."

He couldn't mean that the way it sounded. "Well . . . we could discuss them after you read them."

"I don't have *time* to read, Ruthie," he said as if he were talking to a two-year-old with a hearing problem.

"You could have read tonight," she reminded him.

The look he gave her was a scorcher. "I *thought* our relationship was more important than reading a book. Don't you?"

"Sure, Sean . . . when you put it that way. But I would have understood if you'd stayed home to catch up on your assignment. Or we could have studied together at my house."

"With the monster running loose?"

She laughed. "Yeah, guess you're right."

"So . . . how about it?" He edged over on the seat toward her and touched one of the little tendrils of hair curling around her face. "You're really good at this stuff, Ruthie. Couldn't you help me out this once?"

He was serious! "Sean . . . that would be cheating. You know I can't do that—"

She could tell he knew she was about to cave. And she *was* good in literature, even if she was a total dropout in algebra and biology—

"Please, Ruthie. Pretty please?"

She jumped when he squeezed her shoulder. Then she felt the little dove dangling on the chain around her neck. "If you respected me, you wouldn't even ask, Sean."

He got all huffy then and pulled his hand away. "I'm not talking about *sex*, for Pete's sake!"

"I know. But cheating is wrong, too." Even to her own ears, that sounded so smug, so "I'm-better-than-you-are."

He slumped down further in his seat. "*I* call it helping out a guy who has to work all the time and doesn't want to flunk out of school."

She could feel the distance building between them like a stone wall. It would be so easy. And the poor guy *did* need help. She could just jot down a few notes, and he could use those to write his paper. . . .

Then she remembered something Andy Kelly had said at youth group meeting one time: "*The White Dove program is not just about sexual purity—abstaining from sex before marriage*," he'd said seriously. "*It's about life purity—standing up for what's right, no matter what the circumstances.*"

Even if you have to hurt the one you love the most? she wondered. She could feel the tears beginning to well up in her eyes. In another minute, she'd be blubbering. "I . . . I'm sorry, Sean," she whispered. "I really am."

"I should have known you wouldn't understand," he said sullenly. "You don't know what it's like to have to work and go to school at the same time, and never have time to do it all."

Ruthie caught herself before blurting out that he wasn't the only person who worked full time and still managed to keep up with studies. "I know what it's like, Sean. During the holidays, I keep Justin for Mom and Dad."

"That's not work, Ruthie," he snorted. "That's stuff you do around the house."

"It's the hardest kind of work there is!" she shot

back. Irritated, she stuck to her guns. "And I can't help you, so don't ask me again."

"Okay, so I fail my senior year. You know what that's going to do to me?"

She stuffed her hands in her pockets so he wouldn't see them trembling. "Do you know what it would do to *me* . . . if I cheated? We took a vow, Sean, remember? You took it, too."

"I wasn't asking you to write the paper *for* me—just help me. I don't call that cheating."

She felt a flood of guilt. Isn't that what real friends were for—to help each other out? To stand by when things were tough? Maybe she'd misunderstood. She'd been doing a lot of that lately.

He must have mistaken her silence as the final word, because he changed the subject. "By the way, do you know what Stick wants with me? He's been dogging my trail lately. Even tracked me down to the Pizza Palace the other day."

"The Pizza Palace?" Funny, they usually went there together or with the crowd from school.

He wouldn't look at her but stared through the windshield. "I met some of the guys from work one night, and Stick dropped in and wanted me to go somewhere and talk. But it was kinda late."

Ruthie shrugged, trying to figure out how to avoid telling another lie. "You never really know what Stick has on his mind. Guess you'll have to ask *him*."

Sean let out a long breath as if he'd been holding it, then said in a lethal tone, "You told him about *us*, didn't you?"

"About *us*?" Ruthie squeaked. "Sean, I don't tell

Stick anything—except what a dork he is." By now, she should be prepared for Sean's mood swings, but his accusation shocked her—and scared her. "He saw you let me out at church that night. When you didn't come back for me, he offered me a ride home."

"He what?" Sean all but shouted.

Ruthie cringed, shrinking away from him. "Stick just gave me a ride, that's all. What did you expect me to do?" she asked defensively, hurt that Sean seemed to care so little about her welfare. "Walk home and have some *stranger* try to pick me up?"

"I'll break him in two if he comes near you again, you hear?" Sean's eyes glittered. "That guy can try all the trick shots he wants on the basketball court, but he'd better stay away from my girl!"

When Sean grabbed her wrists and shook her, Ruthie couldn't believe it. He couldn't really be jealous of Stick, could he? He was just upset about that paper he had to write. "Sean, I don't know what's gotten into you. Stick never—"

But before she could finish her sentence, Sean gave her a little shove and she fell back against the door. The minute he let go, she opened the door, jumped out, and ran up the walkway.

"No good-night kiss?"

His mocking question echoed in the night air like a slap.

Sean's hand was trembling when he switched on the engine. Man! What was happening to him? To *them*? Was it really asking so much for Ruthie to help him out? Hadn't he always done the things she'd asked him? He'd gone with her to the youth group, to Sunday school at her church, on youth trips. He'd even gone along with that abstinence vow just to make her happy.

But now, when he needed something from her, what did he get? Nothing! Zilch. A big, fat zero.

Ruthie didn't have a clue about the real world—what it was like to see your family falling apart right in front of your eyes. His mom and dad had always argued a lot. But lately, there had been real shouting matches—that is, when his dad was around. Sean hadn't seen much of his old man since he'd moved into an apartment across town.

Well, Sean wasn't about to run out on Mom. She needed him, even though she was too wrapped up in her own troubles to notice him, except to remind him to "be good" on her way out the door to work or something.

"Be good"? What for? What had being good ever gotten him? A red sports car? A trip to New York? A college scholarship? A girlfriend who cared about what he was going through?

Bummer! Sean raked his hand through the blond hair falling over his forehead. His skin felt hot and sweaty. He'd let himself get too worked up. On top of everything else, he probably wasn't getting enough sleep, either. His dad sometimes dropped by late at night, and his parents went at it again. They'd keep him awake half the night, arguing. They argued about what his dad had done and hadn't done, then passed the blame back and forth. They argued about who was going to get which piece of worthless, old furniture.

But they never argued about which one was going

to get Sean. Didn't even seem to know he was there—let alone care.

The only person in my life who's worth anything is Ruthie—and she's getting more like that uppity crowd every day—having her hair cut, trying to look like a model or something. She cares more about her looks than about helping me write one measly, little paper.

And that one paper meant he would pass or fail. If he failed, he'd be stuck back another year, and Ruthie would be going on to college with the others. Before long it would be "Bye-bye, Sean." Just like Greg Tompkins and Phyllis Haney.

He was sitting there, getting madder by the minute, when it dawned on him where he could get some help. But first, he had to calm down. He leaned over and opened the glove compartment of the car.

Head down, Ruthie hurried up the walk, then eased into the house and closed the door. Only the Christmas tree lights were on in the living room. Justin would already be in bed.

"That you, Ruthie?" her mom called from the kitchen.

"Yeah, Mom. It's me." Ruthie took off her gloves and unzipped her parka. Weird. She hadn't heard Sean drive away.

She turned off the porch light and peeked around the edge of the drape. The car was still parked in the driveway. Why?

While she was watching, she saw a small flash of light inside the car. She could barely make out Sean's silhouette as he leaned over the passenger seat. In the

63

next instant, he straightened up. Another pinprick of light flared red, illuminating his face.

Was Sean *smoking*?

But that couldn't be. Cigarette smoke clung to clothing, car interiors, everything. She'd have noticed the odor, wouldn't she?

Besides, she shouldn't go around expecting the worst of a person. She should have a little faith in him. He *could* have been looking for something. Maybe he'd dropped his car keys and was using one of those tiny keychain flashlights to find them.

Yeah . . . right.

Stick lounged in a front booth of the Pizza Palace, back against the wall, feet propped up on the seat. There were only a few other customers this time of night, and Phyllis Haney, who had come in for the late shift, hadn't even noticed him.

From time to time, he took a sip of his Sprite while reading a novel for an English report—or pretending to read. What he was really doing was looking for Sean. Stick had seen him here that one time last week; maybe he'd luck out again.

He knew Sean was taking Ruthie to the movies to-night. At least that's what Mrs. Jacson had told Stick when he called. It might be a long shot, but he was hoping they'd drop by here afterward, and he could see for himself that everything was cool between the two of them.

With his concentration off, Stick didn't get much reading done. Every time the door opened, he glanced up from his book.

Finally, at 11:30, Sean came in—alone. Stick shut his book and peered over the high back of the seat.

Phyllis, who was at the cash register tallying receipts, greeted Sean with a big smile. "Bud told me to give this to you," she said, reaching into her apron pocket and handing him a small piece of paper. "Said there was more where that came from—if you're interested."

Sean took it and looked down. "I gotta be dreaming! Is this two—"

"Mmm-hmm. You'll notice there's no decimal point between the zeros."

"Wow! Two hundred dollars! There really *is* a Santa Claus."

Stick shuffled to his feet, ready to mosey over and congratulate Sean on winning the sweepstakes or whatever good fortune had come his way. This could be his cue to remind his buddy that even if there wasn't a Santa Claus, there was always God.

That was when he heard Sean say, "And you get—?"

"Twenty percent," Phyllis said, then dropped her voice to a whisper and glanced around furtively. "But let's wait till all the customers have gone."

Sean turned just as Stick stepped up, accidentally elbowing him in the ribs.

"Hey, watch it, ol' buddy. You tryin' to deck your best friend?" Stick thought better of asking what was going on here because Sean was scowling at him as if he were the last person on earth he wanted to see.

"Whatcha doing here? You spying on me again?"

"Sure," Stick said, going along with the joke. "Had nothing better to do."

"Ha! Except stab me in the back."

"Do what?" Stick didn't have the slightest idea what Sean was talking about. On the other hand, he was afraid he *did* have an idea what that faint, musty smell of smoke could be. "I've been trying to get in touch with you for days."

"What for?" Sean growled, his eyes shooting sparks.

"Just wanted to see you, that's all. You've been making yourself scarce lately."

Sean handed Phyllis the slip of paper. "Here, you take care of this." He shucked off his jacket, still glaring at Stick. "Come on. Outside."

"It's cold out there." Sean laughed uncomfortably. "Don't you know this is the coldest spell we've had since—"

Sean flung the door open and barged ahead. "It'll warm up!"

Stick followed. "What's really bugging you, Sean? You want to go for a ride and talk about it?"

"Talk?" Sean grabbed a handful of Stick's basketball jacket, then pushed him—hard. "What would I have to say to someone who's trying to steal my girl?"

Stick did a little back step and stayed on his feet. "Me and *Ruthie*? No way, man. I'm your friend, remember?"

"Some friend!" Sean doubled up his fists.

"This is really dumb, Sean. You expect me to fight you . . . over *nothing*?"

A fist shot out. Stick didn't see it coming, but dodged instinctively and caught only a glancing blow to his right jaw. Still, he braced himself for the next one, automatically spreading his feet and cocking his own fists. Friend or not, a man had to defend himself, didn't he?

For a second, Sean appeared startled that his jab had connected. Then the steam really began to build, and he circled, looking for an opening before letting fly a whole barrage of lightning-fast punches.

At that moment, a car skidded to a stop beside the curb, tires burning rubber. "Hey! What's the trouble here?"

From the corner of his eye, Stick could see a tall black guy jumping out of an old Mustang. Colby! Colby Reid, his old teammate. Reinforcements!

Colby sprang between Sean and Stick, keeping them apart. "Hey, guys, cool it! Can't we talk this over?"

"He didn't *wanna* talk," Stick told Colby, eyeing Sean, who had backed off and was rubbing his knuckles. "But if you change your mind, Sean, my offer's still open."

Holding his jaw, Stick went back inside, where Phyllis was closing up. He dunked a napkin in ice water and held it to his face.

She shot him a murderous look, grabbed Sean's jacket, and rushed out the door.

Six

By the next morning, news of The Fight had spread like an epidemic of Type-A flu.

It was the first thing Ruthie heard when she reached her locker, where Twila, Marcie, and Lana were waiting. Natalie, who would have been with them, was still out of town. "Were the guys *really* fighting over you?" Lana was bug-eyed.

"No wonder," Twila added. "With that jazzy new hairdo, girl, you're the hottest thing since Miss Prissy Cissy took off for the Big Apple!"

Ruthie couldn't help but laugh at the girl's theatrics. *She* was one to talk about hair, with her own head sprouting dozens of tiny black braids. But what kind of story was Twila cooking up? "Whoa. Hold it," Ruthie said, looking at the small group gathered around her. They didn't even budge when the bell rang for first period. "Just *who* was fighting *who—whom*?" she corrected herself.

Marcie squealed. "You don't *know*? It's just so romantic!"

"Wait a minute," Twila interrupted her. "The dumbfounded look on this girl's face is for real. Ruthie, honey, your man is one jealous dude. He walloped Stick good last night."

Ruthie looked from one to the other. "What are you talking about?"

"Well, there's the horse himself," Twila went on, glancing over Ruthie's shoulder. "You might as well get it straight from his mouth."

It was Stick, pausing in his bolt for the classroom. At his approach, the crowd parted to let him through. He looked awful—a cut under his eye, half his face turning an ugly, purplish color.

"Sean didn't call you?" he asked Ruthie.

She shook her head slowly, dazed.

"Well, I just want you to know *I* didn't squeal to the whole world," he insisted. "Wonder who did?"

Twila's round-eyed innocent look was not convincing. "Do *you* know what this is all about?" Ruthie asked her.

"We-ll—" Twila's dark skin flushed even darker. "Colby and I happened to drive by just when the fight started. Sean was shoutin' that Stick here was trying to steal his girl."

"Hey, a fight takes at least two," Stick broke in. "Did you see me throwing any punches?"

"Nope. But that's not grape jelly on your jaw, is it?" Twila giggled. "Maybe you should have used a little more of that fancy footwork you're famous for on the basketball court."

Stick hung his head, and Ruthie couldn't help feeling sorry for him. He was usually the one cracking the jokes around here. But this time, it seemed, the joke was on him.

"Then it wasn't a fight, Twila," he spoke up in his own defense. "Didn't you ever see guys playing around and someone lands a lucky punch? I can't help it that Sean was hacked off because I helped Ruthie get home that night—"

So *that* was it. Sean thought she and Stick had a thing going—just because he'd given her a ride home from church. How could anyone in his right mind come up with such a dumb idea? Especially Sean! But he *had* gone ballistic when he'd heard about it, she remembered. The proof was right there on Stick's face.

No one moved, seemingly unaware that they could all get a warning for being late to class.

Stick suddenly straightened to his full, awesome height and grinned. "If I was trying to steal anyone's girl, I'd at least get a bicycle built for two."

At that, the whole gang erupted in a hoot of laughter.

"Right," Ruthie agreed. "Besides, as anyone can see—I'm not Amy Ainsworth."

After one last suspicious glance at the two of them, Twila shrugged and joined in the laughter. "Maybe that guy of yours is just plain crazy, honey—crazy about *you*!"

Still laughing, the crowd drifted away and on to class as if nothing huge had happened. Ruthie turned to leave, too, not daring to look in Stick's direction. If she did, someone would be sure to make something of it!

Stick had been afraid of this. Last night, when Colby had asked what was up, Stick had tried to explain that it was just a little misunderstanding between pals. Unfortunately, there had been some other eyewitnesses—a few customers at the Pizza Palace who'd run out to see what was going on—not to mention Twila, who was in the car with Colby at the time. This kind of thing had a way of getting around.

True to form, Ruthie had snapped out a denial that there was a shred of truth in Sean's accusation. As long as Amy was around, she'd insisted, no other girl stood a chance.

Cool. Just let 'em believe that. Actually, it had been the biggest coup of his entire career as self-appointed class clown: Guy pines for school beauty while secretly pursuing real passion—basketball. Thinking he was off limits, none of the other girls bothered him, which left lots of time for ball practice—and taking care of Grandpa, of course. He *had* to make good. He owed it to his family.

So ever since he'd laid eyes on Amy, Stick had acted like a certified nut. Of course, he knew dating her was a long shot anyway—her being from the super-strict Ainsworth family and all. She was two years younger and not allowed to go out with boys until she was sixteen. Perfect. By then, he'd have graduated and gotten on with his plans to make it to the pros, earn lots of money, and take care of his mom and Grandpa in style—in that dream house his grandma had always wanted.

Not quite ready to confront Sean, Ruthie was actually relieved when he didn't show up at school. Maybe he'd stayed home to do his reading for English class. And maybe pigs could fly!

After school, though, she was surprised to find that there were no messages for her on the answering machine. If Sean cared enough about her to fight over her, couldn't he pick up the phone and call?

Just at that moment, Justin stepped on her last nerve. "Cut that out! You know Mom doesn't like it when you shake the Christmas presents, then dump them all over the floor."

"The paper's coming off this one," he said, picking up a big, oblong package with his name on it. "Maybe we oughta wrap it again."

"Take your hands off that!" Ruthie lunged for the box, done up in colorful Disney paper. "We'll tape the torn part. Now go watch a video or something. I've got to start supper before Mom and Dad get home."

"On one condition," he said with that calculated gleam in his eye.

She let out a long sigh. "What is it this time?"

"Take me to the basketball game when you go."

"Sure," she agreed. Easy enough. He'd said '*when* you go'; she had no intention of going to tonight's game—not without Sean. "Now put in a video. And make sure it's not one of Mom's."

"Yuck! Who wants to watch that mushy stuff?" He trotted off into the living room, and Ruthie went to the kitchen.

She took the meat loaf out of the freezer, put it into the microwave, and set the timer for "Thaw." Then she peeled potatoes for mashing and put them on to boil. She'd open a can of peas later and toss a salad. Store-bought biscuits would have to do for the bread.

While she was washing up the utensils she'd used, she looked out the kitchen window. Everything seemed so cold and forsaken. A heavy, gray sky threatened ice or snow, and the tree limbs shivered in the wind.

While she was feeling about as low as those clouds out there, the phone rang. She dried her hands on the tail of her T-shirt and reached for it.

"Ruthie, it's Amy," said the familiar voice on the other end of the line. "Are you going to the game tonight . . . because if you are, I can take Sarah and Rose." She didn't pause for breath. "Mom has a night class and Dad's working, and they won't let the girls sit in the stands without supervision. I've got to cheer, of course, or they could sit with me. They're dying to go, but if you're busy or something—"

"Slow down a minute." Ruthie laughed. "To tell you the truth, I hadn't planned to . . . wait—" This could be the perfect solution. If she stayed home, she'd just pig out, then puke up her insides. Why not go to the game and yell her head off instead? "Yeah, I'll go. But there'll be two of us. Me and Mons—Justin."

"There he is! There he is! It's Stick!"

To Ruthie's utter humiliation, her little brother stood up in the bleachers and cupped his hands like a megaphone. "We want Stick! We want Stick!"

Speak for yourself, little bro, Ruthie groused. *I don't want Stick—I want Sean!*

The cheerleaders turned to look in their direction, giggling and whispering, while Ruthie felt her cheeks flush beet red and wished to die. After what had happened between Sean and Stick last night, everyone would think *she'd* put Justin up to this!

But the very next cheer ended with a pyramid, and

as the cheerleader on top dismounted to the floor, they all yelled in unison, "We want Stick! We want Stick!"

From her position in the line, Amy gave Justin the high sign. At that, Justin turned to Ruthie with a satisfied smirk on his face. And soon she, along with the rest of the crowd, was joining in the roar of applause for Shawnee High's finest.

At 6' 6", Stick towered over the other players on both teams. But even though he was long and lanky and a total klutz everywhere else, on the court he was awesome. He could out-dribble, out-score, and out-jump anyone in the state. He'd been voted Shawnee High's MVP every year since ninth grade, and it was rumored he'd be chosen to play on the All-American High School Boys Basketball Team, and after that, on practically any college team of his choice. When he got to the pros, he'd put Garden City, Illinois on the map!

For a while, in the excitement of the game with their long-time rivals, the West High Hornets, Ruthie forgot all about her troubles. It was a tight game— 32–28 at the half, the Hornets ahead. At the end of the third quarter, the Warriors were trailing by two. Everyone went wild when Stick beat the double-team defense and drove for the hoop. But it was a toss-up until, in a burst of speed, he scored one last slam-dunk to lead the team to yet another victory.

Even Amy, who usually wouldn't give him the time of day, was screaming at the top of her lungs, "Go, Stick!" as he was hoisted to the shoulders of Colby and Philip Sloan.

It was only when some of the dating couples paired off to leave that Ruthie felt another pang of self-pity.

What was she doing here, baby-sitting her little brother and the two Ainsworth girls, when she should be with Sean? She really needed to see him, talk to him. Not only about the fight, but about everything else that had been going on lately. But when?

⸻

"Your tree looks great," Ruthie said when she pulled up in front of the Ainsworth house after the game. "I think I like those little white lights better than our colored ones."

The soft glow through the picture window lit Amy's pretty face, putting stars in her eyes. *She looks like an angel or a Christmas present,* Ruthie thought, taking in Amy's fake fur-trimmed white ski jacket over her red cheerleading sweater and skirt. Natalie's younger sister always looked great, but she seemed to sparkle tonight. Maybe it was the season. Or maybe it was *not* having a guy to worry about. Could be there was something to the Ainsworths' strict rules about dating. It sure saved a ton of trouble!

On the other hand, if this was the happiest time of the year, why was Ruthie feeling sorry for herself? "Want to go by the Pizza Palace?" she asked Amy on a whim. "We could see if the gang's there."

"Yeah!" Justin yelled from the backseat, his comment quickly seconded by Sarah and Rose.

"Pipe down, you guys." Ruthie made a face in the rearview mirror. "Who invited *you?* This is a teen thing. You'll get your turn. Besides, we haven't even asked yet."

She had to admit she was more than a little surprised when the Ainsworths not only agreed to let Amy go with

Ruthie, but insisted on keeping Justin for an hour or two. Still, Ruthie *was* Amy's older sister's best friend, and the two families had known each other for eons.

"Thanks, Mr. and Mrs. A.! We'll fasten our seat belts and observe the speed limit." Ruthie cast a skeptical glance at Justin. "Just hope my little brother does the same while we're gone."

She and Amy were still laughing when they reached the Pizza Palace.

"Looks like everyone's here," Amy said when Ruthie pulled into the crowded parking lot.

Inside, while Ruthie looked around for a place to sit, the inevitable happened. Seeing Amy, Stick rushed over, his spiky hair still damp from the shower.

"Table for two?" He bowed deeply, impersonating a waiter, one hand at his waist and the other behind him. "Right this way."

Without waiting for an answer, he marched ahead, plowing a path to a booth in the back. On the way, he managed to bump into a waitress, who was holding a tray of cold drinks over her head. As she was juggling to steady the tray, Stick put out a hand to help, accidentally stumbling against a chair with his size twelve tennis shoe and overturning a glass of Coke.

"Sorry," he mumbled, trying to mop up the mess with a napkin.

But everyone was in a hilarious mood, and since Stick was tonight's hometown hero, no one gave him any grief. Just waved him off and said they'd take care of it.

"Where do you expect us to sit—in your lap?" Ruthie quipped, when they reached the back of the restaurant, crammed with at least half of Shawnee High—

and found only one chair left. "I wouldn't trust you that close to Amy."

"Smart girl," Twila said from her place on the other side of Colby.

Seeing the great-looking couple together made Ruthie miss Sean even more, but she did her best to hide her disappointment.

"Okay, here's a seat for the lady," Stick announced, hauling up a chair from a nearby table. "Now, let's find one for Ruthie!"

She smacked him on the arm.

"Ow!" he moaned. "You ruined my dunking arm."

"You're lucky I don't dunk you in the river—permanently!"

It felt so good to lighten up a little, hear the groans of their friends, the good-natured chuckles.

Ruthie's gaze wandered around the room, where several of the other basketball players were wolfing down pizza with their dates. *I refuse to feel sorry for myself!* she promised and tuned in to the conversation.

"Ready to order?" came a voice at her elbow, and Ruthie glanced up to see Phyllis Haney, pad and pencil in hand.

After giving their order, some of the guys got real quiet. Ruthie couldn't figure it out, but something *felt* different.

Colby leaned over and whispered to Stick, who said, "No way! It's not the time, man!"

"Well, it's sure the place!" Colby was hot. What was going on?

They weren't kidding around with Phyllis like they usually did, either, and she was in a big hurry to take their orders and get out of there. Did this have anything to do with . . . the fight?

"Allow me. Allow me," Stick insisted when Ruthie finally said she and Amy had to go. He rushed to the door and held it open for them, then watched them climb into the car and drive off.

He almost lost his goofy grin after he shut the door and turned to catch Phyllis frowning at him as if she wasn't at all impressed. But he kept the smile plastered on his face and returned to the table, where Colby was ordering another pizza.

Although Stick would have preferred to leave, maybe call Ruthie and find out what was going on with Sean, he stuck around. His bike was tucked away in Colby's trunk, and after using up all that energy on the game, he didn't think he should attempt the long ride home in the cold wind.

They stayed until closing time. As Colby pulled out onto the main road, another car was turning into the parking lot. Stick recognized the driver. It was his ol' buddy Sean.

Right now, all Sean could think about was seeing Phyllis again. She seemed to be the only one who really cared what was happening in his life. She understood. And the *last* thing she'd say was some dumb thing like, "Just pray, and it'll all work out."

This was real life—not that dream world where Ruthie lived—she and her other friends from the youth group. If you wanted things to work out, you had to *make* 'em work. Phyllis knew that. So did her brother and the other guys at work.

Besides, what Sean was doing right now was only temporary. He was preparing for the future. That's what a guy had to do if his dreams weren't handed to him on a silver platter, the way they were for some people he knew.

He drove around to the back and parked. When he banged on the locked door, Phyllis let him in. She seemed real glad to see him.

"Got a minute, Phyll?" he asked. "I need your advice on a couple things."

"Sure." She opened the door wider. "Whatever I can do. By the way, your friends were in tonight."

"Friends?"

"Yeah. You know . . . the basketball team—some of the guys you used to hang out with. And I saw Ruthie and"—she grinned slyly—"the nosy guy you punched out."

Ruthie and Stick! Sean tried to ignore the sudden streak of hot fire that shot through him. "Friend, yeah," he snorted. "With friends like that, who needs enemies?"

She nodded, her eyes flashing with understanding. And sympathy.

Everything was going to change. And soon. They'd see. They'd all see.

He rammed his hand into his pocket, and his fist clenched around the roll of bills, a little larger tonight than usual. Yep, things were definitely going to change.

Seven

On Wednesday night, Natalie called. "Ruthie, I'm home! You've got to come over. It seems like forever since we've talked—I mean really talked."

"Mom and Dad have gone to a party, so I'll have to bring the Monster. Is there someone home who can sit on him?"

"Oh, my dad'll handle your little brother. Just hurry!"

Ruthie found her mom's car keys and drove the few blocks to the Ainsworth's. Natalie was the very one who could help her make sense of this craziness with Sean and Stick.

The Ainsworth Christmas tree, twinkling in the window, was like a welcome sign as Ruthie drove up and parked next to the curb in front of the house. A stiff wind pushed Ruthie and Justin up the walk. At the door, she knocked lightly.

Justin didn't wait for an answer, but barged past her into the house. At Natalie's shriek, Ruthie wondered if her rambunctious little brother had already knocked over the Christmas tree or something.

"I've missed you!" Natalie threw her arms around

Ruthie and gave her a big hug. Then, stepping back, she took another look. "Ruthie Ryan, what have you done to your hair? I love it! You look so grown-up—so uptown."

"I do?" Ruthie felt her cheeks heat up. Her freckles were probably standing out like a case of the measles.

"Hey, listen to this," Justin demanded, calling attention to himself.

Mr. Ainsworth and Sarah politely halted their checker game. Mrs. A. looked up from her bowl of popcorn. Amy continued towel-drying her hair, but glanced his way. And little Rose smiled sweetly, her scissors poised over a magazine picture she was cutting for a homemade Christmas card.

"What reptile was a writer?" He snickered. "Besides Ruthie, I mean."

"Have you been poking your nose in my diary again?" she blared, ready to whack him one.

"Nope. It was locked."

"Okay, Justin," Mr. A. encouraged. "What reptile was a writer?"

"Snakespeare! Get it? Did ya get it? I made that one up myself."

"Never would have guessed," Mr. A. said good-naturedly, returning to his game.

Staring at a nativity set on a table across the room, Justin was suddenly serious. "Something doesn't look right over there. Where's Baby Jesus?"

"We're going to put Him in the manger on Christmas morning," Rose told him.

"Well, it looks funny. I don't like it," Justin said sullenly.

"Oh, try to overlook my little bro. He's such a . . ." Ruthie trailed off, rolling her eyes.

The Ainsworths just laughed. For some reason, they seemed to enjoy Justin's dumb comments. Maybe it was because they didn't have a boy in the family. But they were always like that—only seeing the good in other people.

"We'll be upstairs," Natalie told her family and led the way to her little attic room over the garage.

As soon as they closed the door behind them, Ruthie shucked off her jacket and curled up on the bed.

"You've lost weight, Ruthie," Natalie observed.

"Great. Mission accomplished." Ruthie turned, trying to see her reflection in the dresser mirror. "I've been working on it."

"But why? You didn't need to lose."

"Oh yes, I did. I was getting too fat."

"Says who?"

Ruthie almost slipped up and said, *Says Sean*, but she wasn't ready to get into all that . . . yet. "Says *me*."

"Well, it's only your imagination talking. But I know how you feel. Last summer when I went to the lake with Cissy and Scott and put on a bathing suit, I felt as big as a barn."

"Oh, your figure's just right, Nat. And I like the way you're wearing your hair, too—a little longer and curled under like that."

"Thanks. It was Cissy's idea." Natalie handed Ruthie a pile of brochures and snapshots of New York.

Ruthie flipped through them, then tossed a pillow toward the headboard and propped herself against it. "Now, tell me everything. Did you take a bite out of the Big Apple . . . and was there a worm in it?"

Natalie's big grin spoke volumes. "I'm not sure where to start." She perched on the edge of the bed, near the foot. "Guess I'll start with Cissy."

"Umm . . . leaving the best till last?"

Natalie's smile broadened. "First of all, Cissy *didn't* win the competition."

Ruthie's mouth fell open. "You've got to be kidding! She lost . . . and you're *glad*?" What was wrong with this picture? Natalie always wanted the best for other people.

"Cissy's fine with it, Ruthie. She doesn't quite understand why God let her be in the top ten, then not win. But she's learning to trust Him even when things don't make sense. On the other hand," Natalie added quickly, "Cissy's no loser. After all, she did win the trip to New York City and a gift certificate from Macy's."

"Right." Ruthie paused, remembering that Cissy had been wearing sunglasses the day of the parade. "You mentioned that she'd been hit in the eye with a video camera or something. Do you think her injury could have kept her from winning?"

Natalie shrugged, reached for a throw pillow, and hugged it to her. "Actually, her black eye attracted a lot of attention . . . from some very interesting people, I might add." She grinned again. "Her new boyfriend, for one."

Ruthie sat up straighter. "New boyfriend?"

"The guy who accidentally hit Cissy with his camcorder—Antonio Carlo—is the son of the owners of the Top Ten Modeling Agency. He's a few years older—out of college already. Very good-looking, very charming, very Italian—" Natalie waited for Ruthie's piercing shriek to die down. "*And* he'll be coming to see Cissy before Christmas."

"Wow! Cissy's not only a winner . . . I'd say she hit the jackpot!"

"Yeah. He's coming"—her voice lost a little of its enthusiasm—"with Scott."

"What do you mean, 'He's coming with Scott'? Didn't Scott come home with you and Cissy?"

Natalie shrugged. "Scott was discovered by the agency."

"What? Natalie Ainsworth, you tell me this minute what's going on!"

"The modeling agency noticed Scott, liked what they saw, and signed him up. It's as simple as that."

"Wow," Ruthie breathed. She couldn't quite read her friend's expression—somewhere between being really glad for Scott and sad for herself. So the sane, sensible, always-in-control Natalie Ainsworth really was in love. Nat might not be as glamorous as Cissy or as beautiful as her sister Amy, but she looked pretty terrific with those stars in her eyes. "Then where does that leave *you*?"

"Out in the cold in a way."

Ruthie could relate to that.

Natalie got all breathless. "But I'll never forget our last night in New York, Ruthie." She got up and drifted over to the dresser like a sleepwalker, lifted a box out of a shopping bag, then floated back to the bed. She opened the box, took out the contents, and carefully removed the Styrofoam packing.

"This is Scott's Christmas present from me . . . so

he'll never forget that night. I bought it for him before we left."

It was a snow dome—one of those glass balls with fake snow that swirls around when you shake it. This one contained a tiny replica of the Empire State Building. Ruthie watched as Natalie shook the ball gently, sending the flakes flying about the building.

"Ruthie, it was so beautiful—Scott and I standing on top of one of the tallest buildings in the world, telling each other we love each other, with the snow falling all around us. . . ."

Ruthie gasped but waited for Natalie to finish.

"Scott even suggested we do what the characters did in an old movie—meet in that same spot when we graduate from college—that is, if we still feel the same."

Ruthie was stunned. Natalie was too smart to agree to something like that. "You're not going to, are you?"

Natalie nodded. "How could I refuse? We'll either meet . . . or we'll send word that we've changed our minds."

Ruthie blinked away a tear. "How romantic," she whispered, watching the snow inside the glass bubble and thinking of Sean.

Natalie put the gift away. "Now, I want to hear all about you and Sean, Ruthie. You know, I never really understood before why you two wanted to go steady"—she flashed a sheepish grin—"but I do now."

Ruthie stalled for time, picking at an imaginary speck on her jeans. A good friend wouldn't spoil things by spilling her own troubles. "Sean and I aren't seeing much of each other right now. He only has Wednesday and Thursday nights off. It's bugging him and . . . we've been fussing a lot when we're together. He hates having to work nights."

"Sounds like Dad's job," Natalie said, shifting her position at the end of the bed. "As a prison guard, his hours change every three months, you know. And when he pulls the night shift, he has to work all night every night."

Ruthie pretended to be studying Natalie's snapshots again. But she was thinking that Mr. Ainsworth's hours didn't affect his disposition any. He was always the same—the nicest guy you'd ever want to meet, even when he'd worked all night. But Mr. A. was a wonderful Christian who really practiced what he preached. As for Sean . . .

Natalie seemed puzzled when Ruthie didn't speak up right away. "Looks like we're in the same boat," she went on. "Both our boyfriends are working. But at least yours is in town."

Ruthie perked up a little. There was always hope. "But yours is a *model*. Wow! I always thought Scott was gorgeous, but now his picture will be all over, and you'll get to show him off to the whole world!"

Natalie frowned. "That's what I'm afraid of. He'll belong to everyone—not just to me." Then her frown lines disappeared, and the old optimistic Nat was back. "But right now, everything's perfect."

The more she raved, the more Ruthie felt like crawling into the woodwork. Not only was Scott the "sweetest, kindest, most considerate guy in the world," but Natalie was singing Cissy's praises, too. "She's really changed, Ruthie. You know how we used to

think she was such a snob? Well, now she's more concerned about everyone else than she is about herself.
That's one reason losing the competition didn't bother
her. And, Ruthie"—Natalie leaned closer as if the next
news was almost too good to be true—"Cissy asked me
to be her friend."

"Uh . . . great." Now that *was* the last straw! If
Natalie had stuck a knife in Ruthie's ribs, it couldn't
have hurt any worse. Maybe Sean was right—about
some things, at least. Looked like Natalie was "moving
up" with the rich set.

There was an awkward silence before Natalie
shifted gears. "Has Sean decided where he's going to
college, or what he wants to do after graduation?"

Ruthie shrugged. "A lot depends on *whether* he
graduates. If he makes a failing grade on his English
paper, I wouldn't be surprised if he dropped out of
school." She stopped short of telling Natalie that Sean
had asked her to write the paper for him. There was no
doubt what Nat would say to *that*. Cheating was
wrong. That's all there was to it.

Ruthie couldn't hide the edge in her voice when she
went on coolly, "As for what he wants to do, he just
says he definitely doesn't want to be a grease monkey
like his dad."

"Well, that's a start."

"A start of what?"

Natalie stared at her strangely. "Of . . . choosing a
career. I mean, elimination is part of the process. If he
knows he doesn't want to work at a service station,
then that's something."

"Is it?" Ruthie asked dully. She didn't like the

direction this conversation was taking—like Natalie was comparing Sean to Scott or something. Not every guy had a career handed to him before he was even out of high school, for Pete's sake.

"*You* know . . . like Thomas Edison," Natalie went on. "When his assistant said they'd failed to invent the incandescent light bulb, Edison said, 'No, we haven't failed. We know two thousand things that don't work.' "

Ruthie sniffed. "Well, I wouldn't say Sean has failed just because he doesn't want to work at a service station."

"I didn't mean it that way, Ruthie," Natalie spoke up defensively, then squinted at her. "Did . . . something happen while I was in New York?"

"Like what?"

"Well, Amy said she heard rumors."

"What rumors?" Ruthie snapped.

"Like . . . Sean and Stick fighting over you."

"Oh, Natalie, you know how those things get started. Yeah, Sean and Stick had a few words and Sean punched him, but it wasn't about *me*," she hedged. "You know what Stephanie and Andy say about gossip spreading like wildfire. . . ."

She deliberately changed the subject. "Oh, did you hear about Stick? Some colleges and universities are already after him. They say they'll offer a full four-year scholarship if he keeps playing as well as he is now. Can you believe it? Stick Gordon—sports celeb!"

Natalie laughed. "I've always said Stick isn't half as bad as you think."

"Well, he's a good basketball player, all right. But

. . . you know Stick." She lifted her hands.

"Sarah thinks he makes a lot of sense."

Ruthie sighed. "Then she knows something I don't!" She regretted that comment the minute it left her tongue. She'd always kidded around about Stick. Lately, she had to admit, she'd seen a different side of him. For one thing, he actually seemed to care about what was happening with her and Sean.

Glancing at her watch, Ruthie saw that it was getting late. She had to get Justin home. She swung her feet onto the floor. "Nat, would you pray for us—for Sean and me?"

"Sure I will. . . ." Natalie hesitated a minute. "Ruthie, I know Sean is working and has family problems, and that could account for his not showing up for church much. But do you know if he's ever accepted Jesus as his Lord and Savior?"

Ruthie could only shake her head miserably. "I've been wondering about that, too. But I didn't want to push him. You know, Sean doesn't come from a Christian family like ours, so he doesn't know much about . . . church stuff. I guess I expected it to grow on him." She stared off into space. "I've failed him, Nat," she wailed. "I've let him down . . . the one who's supposed to love him the most!"

"Stop that right now, Ruthie. You don't love Sean the most—*God* does. Let's pray."

Before Ruthie knew what was happening, Nat had begun: "Thank you, Lord, for the tough times"— Ruthie glanced up in surprise, then bowed her head again as Natalie continued—"when we don't have anywhere else to go but to you. You're the only One with

the answers to what Sean should do with his life . . .
what Ruthie and Sean should do about their relationship . . . to what's going to happen when we all graduate. . . ." When Natalie paused, Ruthie thought the
prayer was coming to an end, but there was more. "So
help us focus on you instead of on our problems. Help
us to know that you loved us so much you gave up
heaven and came to earth as a baby to save us. And
help us to love *you* most of all. In your name, Amen."

It was a neat prayer, but Ruthie couldn't take much
more. "Gotta go." She forced a weak smile, ran down-
stairs and grabbed Justin on the way out, and high-
tailed it to the car before she broke down in front of
Nat and her family.

On the way home, Justin was still griping about the
Ainsworths' manger scene. "It just didn't look right.
The Baby Jesus belongs in there."

"What's really bad, Justin," Ruthie said, trying to
swallow over the lump in her throat, "is when people
don't have Jesus where He really belongs—in their
hearts."

Out of the corner of her eye, she could see her little
brother's head jerk around. He stared at her for a long
time, then turned toward the window and didn't say
another word the rest of the way home.

With Justin keeping his mouth shut for a change,
Ruthie had time to think. Nat had stuck by Scott all
during that awful ordeal with his mom's alcoholism
and his brother's drunk driving accident at the lake.
Now she was even willing to wait for him while he pur-
sued a modeling career, followed by four years of college. Scott, at least, shared Natalie's belief in Jesus,
while Sean . . .

Sean and I just can't break up! Ruthie groaned. *Not now—when he needs me more than ever.* Then a horrible thought crossed her mind. *But what if he* doesn't *need me anymore? What if he's found someone else?*

Eight

The following Wednesday morning, Sean called before Ruthie left for school. "Look, sorry I haven't been around. I've had a lot on my mind, but I'll tell you all about it later. For the next few days, though, I'm only planning to go to classes I have exams in. Pick you up tonight for the youth group meeting?"

The jerk! she fumed to herself. *If he thinks he can hop in and out of my life like that, he has another thing coming!* "Actually, I'd planned to go with Natalie," she said, as casually as she could manage.

"Oh, so your friend is back from the big city, and now you're running around with that high-falutin' crowd!" he snorted. "I guess I know where that leaves *me!*"

Ruthie mumbled something about seeing him later and hung up. Just when she'd promised herself—and God—that she was going to try to be a better influence on Sean, she'd blown it. Totally frustrated, she went into the kitchen and rummaged around in the cookie jar. *My body is God's temple, but I don't think He minds if I have one little cookie—even if Sean does. I'm not going to starve myself over a guy!*

She'd barely made it to school before Marcie intercepted her in the hall. "I probably shouldn't tell you this, Ruthie, but I thought you ought to know. I've heard it from two different people that Sean's been going to the Pizza Palace every night after work."

"What about it, Marcie? He gets off work long past my curfew."

"Yeah, but . . . there's more. He's been seen leaving with Phyllis . . . after she closes up on the late shift."

"Phyllis?"

"You know . . . Phyllis Haney. She's a waitress at the Pizza Palace."

Ruthie recalled the Friday night when a deathly hush had settled over the whole table after Phyllis had come to take their order. Did everyone else know something she didn't know? That Sean preferred older women—Phyllis Haney, to be exact? *Why doesn't he have the guts to tell me himself?* Ruthie wondered. *Lately he seems to get a kick out of tormenting me.*

But he *had* said they'd talk soon—and that she'd understand everything.

Oh, great. Today is probably going to be "Drop Ruthie" day!

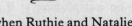

That night, when Ruthie and Natalie arrived in the church parking lot, Stick was standing near the door. Ruthie wondered if Stick had forgotten all about the little fiasco when Sean had shoved her out of his car. Probably, knowing Stick. All he thought about was basketball. And Amy Ainsworth. Period.

For a moment, Ruthie felt a little guilty for turning

down Sean's offer of a ride. Now, if he didn't come to youth group, it would be *her* fault. How had things gotten so weird?

She might as well face it—it was over between her and Sean. He wasn't the least bit interested in her anymore—no matter what he said.

That's why she was so surprised when Sean came in late to the meeting, carrying a huge pink poinsettia, and steering a path in her direction. At first, she figured the plant must be for one of the single parents.

But she was wrong.

"Merry Christmas," he said softly, handing her the plant and giving her one of those long, slow looks that always made her knees weak.

"For *me*?" She couldn't believe it. How could she have been so wrong about him? "Sean, you shouldn't have." He had to work so hard; he really shouldn't be spending his money on flowers for her.

She caught Stick watching from across the room. For the first time since she could remember, there was no goofy grin on his face—only a skeptical look, as if he wasn't quite sure what to make of this. He was probably thinking of the night Sean had left her stranded. But Sean was making up for it tonight, wasn't he?

Right now he was looking as if he wanted to say more, but he just smiled and went to go help Stick fill a box with canned goods. Nat was smiling, too, so she obviously didn't see anything strange going on.

Then an ugly little thought crept in to ruin everything. If this was Ruthie's Christmas present from Sean, why had he made a public spectacle of it? Why not give it to her privately? Was he trying to prove something?

On the other hand, he'd *tried* to see her. She was the one who had turned him down for tonight. So what else could he do? Still . . .

Nat interrupted her thoughts. "I suppose you'll be riding home with Sean, won't you?"

"Nope." Ruthie had made up her mind. "He's got to learn my love's not for sale. I'm really tired of fussing and making up. How do I know it won't happen again? Besides, I *came* with you and I'm *leaving* with you."

When she told Sean as much, she thought he would explode. But instead, he only ducked his head, then peeked at her again, looking not a day older than *Justin*. "Okay . . . but I'll miss you."

For a minute, she almost changed her mind. Sean could be so sweet when he wanted to be, and she loved him as much as ever. But she wasn't ready to stick her neck out again, only to get it chopped off. And there were a few things they had to get straight—like Phyllis Haney. . . .

On the way home, Nat was unusually quiet—even for Natalie. "Ruthie, you know I don't like to repeat gossip," she finally said.

Ruthie decided to make it easier for her. "But you've heard something about Sean, and you want to know if it's true." When Natalie nodded, she sighed. "It'll take a while. Can you come in?"

Inside, Ruthie set Sean's poinsettia on the coffee table for her family to admire while Natalie called to let her parents know she'd be late. Then Ruthie led the way to her bedroom, where she settled herself on the bed and unloaded the whole nine yards on Nat. Sean's mood swings. His shoving her out of the car that frigid night. His biting her head off over the least little thing. The fight with Stick. And now . . . Phyllis!

"Everything is such a mess!" Ruthie wailed. "I was thinking of dumping Sean before he dumps me. Then he brings me a Christmas present in front of half the church. Nat, what am I going to do with that guy?" She felt for the little dove around her neck. "He needs . . . a whole lot more than I can give him."

Natalie didn't say anything for minute. "I'm not sure anyone else could have done any better, Ruthie. Sean has to make his own decision about trusting the Lord with his life, you know."

"Yeah, but maybe I could have done *something*." She heard a rustle behind her and turned to find Justin standing in the doorway. "Justin Ryan! Were you eavesdropping?"

His face clouded over. "I didn't drop nothing."

Natalie stifled a giggle, and Ruthie sighed. "What do you want?"

"I wanted to ask Natalie if they'd put Baby Jesus in the manger yet."

"Not until Christmas morning, Justin," Nat explained patiently. "It's what Advent is all about really—counting the days until Jesus' birthday."

Justin's eyes flashed, and he put his hands on his hips. "Well, something's missing in your manger scene, if you ask me!"

"That really seems to be getting to him," Natalie observed as he stalked away.

"Oh, don't worry. He'll get over it." Ruthie was

impatient to get back to the subject of Sean. "What do you think I should do about my guy?"

"I can't tell you what to do," Nat said, gazing off into space with a worried little frown on her face, "but I do know he shouldn't be getting physical like that. When Scott was going through his family crisis, he never took it out on me. For a while, he had some doubts that things were going to turn out okay for his mom and Zac, but he kept on believing that God was in control."

"That's what bothers me, Nat. I don't think Sean has a clue about all that. Oh, he comes to church with me sometimes, but I'm pretty sure he's never turned his whole life over to the Lord."

Natalie shook her head. "He's been exposed to the truth . . . but it just didn't take. Think you should ask Andy and Stephanie to talk to him?"

"Maybe." Still holding tightly to the little dove, Ruthie took a deep breath. "But I need to talk to him first."

———

The opportunity to confront Sean came sooner than Ruthie expected. She was putting her books in her locker when Sean rushed up, all excited. "You'll never believe it! Take a look at this!"

He shoved a paper under her nose. In spite of all the red marks, there was a big "C" at the top of the page. It was a decent grade, so why did she have a sneaking suspicion that he hadn't had time to read the books before he prepared his report? "That's great, Sean. I'm really glad for you."

Ignoring the other kids hurrying past them on their

way to classes, Sean grabbed her hands. "Now that I've passed, let's celebrate!"

Ruthie couldn't resist a snide remark. "Sure you wouldn't rather celebrate with Phyllis?"

Sean turned pale—from shock or guilt?

"Well? You're not answering me," she said in an accusatory tone.

Color flooded his face, and his eyes sparked with anger. "Who's been talking to you? Stick! Right?"

"You want me to say yes so you can punch him out again?" she blazed in return.

"I'm right! It *was* Stick!"

"Wrong! Stick hasn't said a word to me about you. Why did you have that fight with him anyway?"

"He's been bugging me, Ruthie—acting like he's your guardian angel or something."

"He's your *friend*, Sean," she reminded him, giving him a withering look. "Or he used to be."

"Well . . . I apologized. What more can I do?"

"You can answer my question, for one thing. Are you going out with Phyllis or not?'

The look on his face told her all she needed to know.

"I didn't want to say anything, Ruthie. I knew you'd only get the wrong idea. She . . . helped me with my English paper, that's all."

Her heart sank. "I told you I'd help you."

"Yeah, but when? You've got cantata practice on Saturday mornings and church on Sundays. Time was running out. I had to do something fast." His eyes brightened. "But things are beginning to work out, Ruthie. So . . . how about it? Can we go somewhere a week from tonight? I've got some great news."

Before she could answer him, a shadow darkened his smile. "Who knows when we can get together again. On my next days off, Mom and I are going to my grandparents' house. And I don't know what I'll be doing on Christmas Day."

"You won't have to work, will you?"

"I'll be off Christmas Eve, but I'll have to work Christmas night. Gotta load the trucks so they can get to the stores the day after. Some jobs don't take a time out just because there's a holiday, you know."

Yeah. Natalie's dad, a prison guard, had a job like that. "Okay then, we're on for next Thursday night. But I've got to run. I'll be late to class." The halls were almost empty now.

He nodded and winked, his sunny self again. "Cool! On the chance you'd say yes, I made reservations at Crystal's. So wear your neatest outfit—that green thing that shows off your great figure."

On the way to class, Ruthie was still shaking her head. "I wish he'd make up his mind," she muttered. "One day I'm too fat; the next, I've got a 'great figure.' One minute he condemns me for running around with the ritzy crowd; the next, he's making reservations for the fanciest restaurant in town! Whatever happened to the guy I thought I knew?"

After school the following Thursday, Ruthie picked up the phone and dialed Natalie. "Pray for me," she asked her friend. "Sean was in such a good mood all day, he just might be plotting something crazy for to-night—like breaking up or something. And if not, I'm just going to have to do it myself. I'm getting dizzy from this emotional roller coaster ride!"

Nine

The Crystal Restaurant was fabulous—like a winter wonderland, all in silver and white.

From the ceiling of the room hung a huge crystal chandelier, its thousands of glass prisms sparkling in the soft light. On the walls, crystal globes shimmered. Round tables, skirted in white, were placed about the room, with curtained booths on two sides. In the center of each table, candles flickered in crystal candelabra. Wow! A scene straight out of the movies!

Seeing all the other customers in their holiday finery, Ruthie was beginning to wish she'd chosen something a little more festive than her second-best Sunday dress. But it was the one Sean liked best—a shade of green that complemented her red hair. Besides, it was just right with his casual look: dress shirt—no tie— khaki pants, and sweater. But Sean would look great in anything!

The maitre d' led them to one of the curtained booths, where heavy white fabric draperies were pulled back on either side with silver tassels. Inside, the booth was very private and *very* romantic. It was like being in their own little world.

How would Sean pay for all this? The bill was going to be huge!

Across from her, he was already studying one of the oversized menus the waiter had brought. Ruthie tried to relax and sipped her water, lulled by the classical music playing in the background and the low hum of voices outside their booth. This was probably the most grown-up thing she'd ever done, and she might as well enjoy it.

She picked up her own menu, determined to find something cheap. But there were no prices listed in the margin beside the elegant-sounding entrees. Uh-oh. Didn't this mean that everything was super-expensive and the host was the only one with a price list? But Sean didn't seem worried. Maybe the food warehouse had given him a really good Christmas bonus.

He'd said something about exchanging Christmas presents tonight. Well, she had his—a new cable-stitch sweater to match his eyes. She'd left it out in the car for him to open later. No doubt this dinner was his gift to her—especially since he'd already given her a beautiful poinsettia. Well, this evening was a terrific present . . . unless he intended to dine her, then drop her! With Sean acting so weird lately, that was a distinct possibility.

She sneaked a peek at him to see what kind of mood he was in. "This is all really wonderful, Sean."

He grinned, his dimple flashing in his left cheek. In the candlelight, with those little flecks of green glinting in his gray eyes, he looked more handsome than ever. "Wish we could do things like this more often."

"Oh, Sean!" Didn't he know she didn't want

anything except his love—and to be treated nicely, the way he used to treat her.

"Have you decided what you want to order?"

There was no telling about these prices, and she sure didn't want to do the wrong thing. Besides, that day at McDonald's, when she'd mentioned ordering a salad, he'd hooted at her. "Since you've done such a terrific job of planning this evening so far," she said, "why don't you order for both of us?"

Whew! It must have worked, because he cocked one eyebrow. "You sure?"

"Oh, it *all* looks so delicious that I'd never be able to decide." She smiled her sweetest smile. They might end up with a crust of bread, but at least it would be served in style.

When the waiter came, Sean ordered the same for both of them. "Filet mignon with baked potato and asparagus with Hollandaise, please. Oh, and bring us the salad with shrimp and artichoke hearts."

Ruthie swallowed hard. There had to be at least ninety thousand calories in all that food! She'd been working so hard to lose weight recently. In fact, she was pretty proud of herself; she'd lost quite a few pounds. But if she wasn't careful, she'd put every one of them back on with this one meal!

While she picked at her salad—neither of them had ever eaten artichoke hearts—she was grateful when Sean steered the conversation to fairly safe topics: school, the basketball season, his job. He'd never really liked working at Little Egypt. The hours were long, and the pay was minimum wage. Plus, the work was back-breaking: unloading cartons and crates at the dock, then stocking shelves with the heavy cans and jars.

But there was at least one fringe benefit—the workout he got. Even under his wool sweater, Sean's biceps bulged, and his neck looked thicker. *Wow!* Ruthie thought. *Wonder if that sweater I bought him for Christmas is going to fit?*

He looked so great and was acting so sweet, she almost forgot to eat, and she wasn't even through with her salad when the waiter brought their entrees, served on silver chargers. The food was delicious, but she could only choke down a few bites. What if Sean was leading up to a big letdown?

Still, better to know the worst and get it over with. Besides, Ruthie was sick of tiptoeing around the truth. Weren't Andy and Stephanie Kelly always urging the youth group to be honest with one another?

"Sorry I got so bummed about Phyllis," she began, testing the waters. "I'll understand if you decide you'd rather go out with . . . other people . . . than go steady with me."

"Ruthie, get real!" He seemed shocked. "You're the only girl for me."

His expression was so sweet and his tone so sincere, she relaxed a little more. It was super to have the old Sean back—the guy she knew and loved—though his mood could shift with the speed of lightning. "Thanks for the beautiful poinsettia. I've never had one of my own."

"Glad you like it." She couldn't tell, but he seemed to be laughing at her—like he knew something she didn't know. What was he up to? "Oh, and thanks for tonight, too. This is probably the best Christmas present you could have given me . . . an evening to remember. . . ." *Might be the last one*, she couldn't help thinking.

"Who says this is your Christmas present? Or the flower, for that matter?"

"But . . . I thought. . . ." She was genuinely puzzled. He had already spent way too much on her.

She watched as he reached inside the pocket of his shirt and pulled out a small, square box wrapped in silver paper and tied with a fuchsia bow. It looked like a custom gift wrap—from some exclusive store.

What in the world could it be? Earrings? A new chain for her white dove pendant?

Her hand was trembling as she accepted the package. She tore off the wrapping and lifted out a small jeweler's box. She glanced over at Sean, her heart pounding ninety miles an hour.

He nodded. "Go ahead. Open it."

Trembling big time now, she lifted the hinged lid. Nestled against the black velvet was a ring. A *ring*? It was kind of small, but it had to be one of those cubic zirconia deals, cut to look like a real diamond. It couldn't be a *real* one.

"Sean?" she croaked. "This . . . isn't what it looks like, is it?"

"What's it look like?"

"A . . . a diamond."

"Think I'd give you glass?"

"No, but . . . what does it mean? Is it a pre-engagement ring or what?"

"No, stupid. No 'pre' about it. It's an engagement ring."

She couldn't hide the tears that sprang to her eyes. *There he goes again! Calling me 'stupid' and asking me to marry him, all in the same breath. How is that supposed to make me feel?*

In the next minute, she was remembering how many times she'd done the same thing—said something that had hurt someone—her little brother, Stick, no telling how many others. Still, she'd never expected to be called names the night she got engaged.

She swiped at her eyes. Maybe, in the dim light, he wouldn't notice she was about to cry. Or he might just put it down to female emotions. In the awkward moment, she blurted out the first thing that came to mind. "But how could you afford it?"

He was mad, she could tell. "I have a job, remember?" he said shortly. "I've been saving my money. I thought we loved each other—and when two people love each other, they usually get married, don't they?" He frowned and narrowed his gaze. "But maybe you haven't been doing all this slimming down and sprucing up for *me*. Could be you had somebody else in mind."

"Oh, Sean, don't start that again. You know I love you more than anyone else. But aren't we a little young to be thinking about getting married?" Especially when they'd barely been speaking lately. "I'm only seventeen."

"So . . . we don't take any big steps till this summer, when you're eighteen." Without another word, he got up, came around the booth, and slid in beside her. He took the ring from the box and slipped it on her finger.

It was a perfect fit. "H-how did you know my size?"

He leaned over and whispered in her ear. "Easy. Remember when I tried on your class ring, and it fit the knuckle of my little finger?"

The tiny diamond caught the candle glow and winked in the light. This couldn't be happening. It was too soon. She glanced up at Sean, and he pulled her to him and kissed her—hard.

"Sean!" She pushed him away. "This is a public place!"

Actually, the draperies on either side hid them from the view of almost everyone in the room.

"So what? We just got engaged, Ruthie. And you're already sounding like a nagging wife"—his mood shifted again, and he draped his arm around her shoulder—"so let's get to the good stuff." He nuzzled her neck, while she backed away.

"Uh . . . Sean . . . the ring is great . . . and you know I love you . . . but I . . . I wasn't quite ready for this," she stalled. "I need some time to think."

He stiffened and moved his arm. "This is all the thanks I get? I spend my hard-earned money on an engagement ring, and my girl has to *think* about it?"

By this time, he'd returned to his own seat and was glaring across the table at her, his voice raised.

Through the opening, Ruthie could see heads turning in their direction. She didn't dare cause a commotion by taking off the ring and giving it back now. Besides, wasn't this what she wanted? What every girl dreamed of?

Oh, she'd thought about marriage, all right—down the road somewhere. But high school was for having fun—not settling down to babies and budgets and all that adult stuff. It was all happening so fast. But how was she going to make Sean understand what she wanted? And did she even know herself?

"You ready to go?" He was still grumpy, but he did hold her coat and help her into it. With his face very close to hers, he seemed more like the guy she'd loved for two years.

In the car, he switched on a rock station and drove her home without making conversation. But when he pulled up in front of her house, he was all smiles again. And when he walked her to her door, he tilted her face toward his. "You hurry up and think," he said, dropping a tender kiss on her lips. "But your answer better be yes. I'll call you later."

She nodded and waited at the door, staring after him until he reached the car. He lifted his hand in a little salute, and she waved back. Would she ever figure him out?

Still dazed, she stepped inside the front door. Luckily, the living room was empty, but she kept her left hand in her coat pocket in case anyone should walk in.

"It's me, Mom," she said softly.

"Glad you're home, hon," Maureen Ryan called from the kitchen. "I'm in here, finishing up a fruitcake. Come on in and tell me about your big night out."

Ruthie quickly slipped the ring off her finger and dropped it into her pocket. "Want me to unplug the Christmas tree lights?"

"Might as well. But keep your voice down. Justin and your dad are already asleep."

Ruthie heard Sean drive away, and she took a deep breath for courage and walked into the kitchen. "Oh, Mom, that place was incredible," she said, hoping her shaky emotions weren't showing. "It was so sweet of Sean to take me out as part of my Christmas present. And after giving me that beautiful poinsettia. . . ."

Her mother smiled. "He's a nice boy." There was a little pause before she leveled her gaze at Ruthie across the kitchen counter. "But I do hope you're not getting too serious about Sean. He doesn't come from a very stable background, I'm afraid."

Ruthie pretended to ignore the comment and faked a yawn. "It's late. Better get my beauty sleep."

There was absolutely no way *now* she'd tell her mother that "nice boy" wanted to marry her daughter!

It was past midnight when Sean drove to the warehouse and pulled up in back. He was plenty nervous. It was not every night a guy got himself engaged. And on top of that, he had a very important appointment.

Cliff and Bud had promised to meet him here and introduce him to the "big boss"—the one who could guarantee Sean that he could give Ruthie all the fancy dinners, flowers, and jewelry she'd ever want. . . .

Ten

The next morning, Ruthie fastened the diamond ring on the chain with her little dove, made sure it was secure beneath a turtleneck, and pulled on a sweater. Best not to let anyone see it—not even Natalie—because she wasn't anywhere near ready to announce her engagement.

Why not? she had to ask herself. If she really loved Sean, wouldn't she want the whole world to know they were going to get married?

Marriage was a big step. In youth group meetings, the Kellys had led discussions, reminding them that marriage was a lifetime commitment. It sure wasn't anything you jumped into without considering all the consequences.

She glanced down at the jeweler's box lying on her dressing table. Better not leave that lying around. Justin might find it. He could demolish a house quicker than a herd of rampaging elephants.

She'd also heard that some parents even checked their kids' rooms—for drugs and stuff. There was no problem with that, of course, but her mom was already a little suspicious of her feelings for Sean. What if she decided to poke around, found the diary, and read all about Ruthie's bingeing and purging . . . and the ring?

Where could she hide the box where no one would be likely to discover it? *My locker at school!* Yes, she'd leave it there until she could decide what to do.

When she was ready for school, she shoved the jewelry box in the pocket of her jacket. She wouldn't be able to draw a deep breath until it was safely stashed in the back of her locker. *It'd be just my luck, though, if today's the day for a drug search! I can hear the principal now, making a public announcement over the loud speaker: "Which of you students recently got engaged and is not telling?" That's when Sean would report to the office and confess: "I cannot tell a lie. It is I . . . and Ruthie Ryan." Except Sean would be more likely to say, "Me and Ruthie."*

What would she do then?

In the car beside Mom, Ruthie hung on to the box for dear life, praying that nothing would happen on the way to school. The little diamond dangling at the end of her silver chain was as heavy as lead. What if the chain broke? What if the ring came off somehow? What if it burned a hole in her chest?

And what would she tell Natalie when she asked about her date with Sean?

She was jolted back to reality in the hallway at school when Natalie walked up. "Well, I'm dying to know. What happened last night?"

Ruthie jumped as the first bell sounded. *Perfect timing!* she thought as she pushed the little black box to the very back of her locker and slammed it shut. "Sorry, Nat, I can't talk now. Gotta get this last exam out of the way. We'll talk later, okay? Maybe tonight, while we decorate for the single parents' party."

Ruthie pulled up in the church parking lot just as Natalie and her sisters were getting out of their car. A blast of arctic air drove them all toward the basement of the church and into the warmth of the kitchen, where some of the women were busy at work, preparing food for the party.

After peeling off her jacket, Ruthie felt for the chain around her neck to make sure the ring was still securely hidden. But she couldn't help wondering, *If being engaged to Sean is right, why am I so reluctant to tell my best friend?*

There was no time to ponder, though, because Stephanie had spotted them coming in and hurried over to greet them. "Hey, you guys, am I glad to see you! I can put you all to work. Here, Ruthie, you place the napkins—to the left of the plates."

"Cute," Ruthie said, noticing the place cards and the special table reserved for the children—complete with toys.

"Thanks." Stephanie beamed with pleasure. "Each toy is tagged with a child's name, so the children can find their places, eat, and be entertained while their moms—or dads—have some adults-only conversation for a change. Now, Natalie," she continued briskly, "you and your sisters can help Andy trim the tree. He's bringing it in now."

Great! Ruthie heaved a sigh of relief. She still wasn't ready to talk to Natalie, and apparently they'd be busy right up until time for the party to begin.

Natalie and her two sisters pitched in to help string the lights on the big cedar Andy had set up on the stage up front, while Stephanie directed another group of the youth to make and hang stars from the ceiling of the fellowship hall.

As Ruthie walked around the long tables, alternating the red and green napkins on the white cloths, she thought again how well the Kellys worked together. *And the two shall be one*, the Bible said. She remembered that from one of their studies.

Wonder if Sean and I could ever have a marriage like that? Or will he always be so moody and unpredictable that I'd never really know my other half?

"If you're going to the party with me, get a move on," Ruthie was telling Justin when Natalie called, asking for a ride.

"Amy promised to pick up a couple of her friends," Nat explained, "and Mom's taking them early so she can drop off the casseroles she made."

"Fine. I've got Mom's car tonight. But I'll have Justin with me," Ruthie warned, secretly grateful that she wouldn't be alone in the car with her friend.

Natalie laughed. "Oh, Rose can ride with us. She can handle him."

But at the church, Ruthie marveled at the change in her little brother. Like a born leader, he took charge of the smaller children as they arrived, asking their names and finding their place-card toy, cautioning them not to touch anything yet, then leading them over to a corner to show them some picture books. "Wow! What happened to *him*?"

"Don't you know?" Nat asked, chuckling. "It's Christmas!"

The single moms, along with a couple of single dads—relieved to have their children happily occupied—began to mingle and enjoy the evening. A quartet of musicians from the cantata, in costume to advertise the upcoming program, circulated through the crowd, singing carols. The huge Christmas tree, encircled with gaily wrapped gifts, splashed the stage with color, and candles gleamed from the tables. Overhead, stars cut from heavy foil and sprinkled with glitter twinkled in the reflected light.

"Dinner is served, folks, cafeteria-style," Andy announced, stepping up to an on-stage microphone. "Just help yourself, then find your place at one of the tables. There's plenty for all. But before we eat, let's thank the Lord for His provision and for the reason for this season."

After the "Amen," the children, shepherded by some of the youth group members, stormed the serving tables and were then shown to their special reserved table. Fascinated by their new toys, some of them forgot to eat. Ruthie had to laugh. "We'll be sending home lots of doggie bags tonight."

During dessert, Andy made some announcements, thanking the volunteers and those in the youth group who had pitched in to make this event special for all of them. Ruthie felt a little guilty, remembering *her* special evening with Sean. Baked ham and sweet potatoes, served on folding tables, was hardly filet mignon and artichoke hearts at The Crystal! She felt for the little ring, bulging slightly under her sweater, and wished for Sean. . . .

"Now for the surprise we've been promising you. If all the children will gather down front, we have a very special guest—someone who's come a long way to see you. He's very old and very wise, so listen carefully to everything he has to say."

With that introduction, a tall man made his way toward the front of the room. He was wearing a long purple velvet robe, a gold crown on his head. His long gray hair and beard fell nearly to his waist, and he appeared dignified and regal . . . until his foot, covered in a huge tennis shoe beneath his robes, tripped on the second step and he had to scramble to keep his balance.

Ruthie couldn't control an involuntary snicker. Anyone who knew Stick Gordon would recognize him now—even in that getup. Only *he* could have blown his cover that way. But the children didn't seem to mind and gazed up at him with wonder in their eyes.

His dignity intact, Stick managed to walk over and sit down beside Andy, folded his hands, and tried to look wise.

Andy started the questioning. "Can someone tell me just who is a wise man?"

"He's somebody that's not stupid," Justin piped up.

Andy gave a wry smile. "You might say that . . . but what does the Bible tell us about the wise men?"

A little girl raised her hand. "They're the ones who took presents to Baby Jesus."

"That's right. But maybe you'd rather hear the story from the wise man himself."

Stick, his full sleeve draping dramatically as he gestured, pointed toward the ceiling, where the homemade stars danced and glittered in the candlelight. "It was a star just like one of those—only bigger and brighter," he began in a deep, surprisingly rich voice, "that my friends and I saw in the East. We followed it for many months."

The children listened with rapt attention as he described the camel ride across desert sands—looking for relief from the blistering heat of day and shivering in the bitterly cold nights. "But we had only one goal in mind—to find the newborn Son of God."

Ruthie leaned forward in her seat. She'd never seen this side of Stick. So far, he was great. But sooner or later, he'd be sure to goof up. Or crack a joke. But though she listened to every word, not once did he break up. Awesome. The story was obviously his spin on the original version, but he made it seem so fresh and new that she actually felt she was *there*, experiencing that holy night.

"Who knows why the wise men gave gifts to Baby Jesus?" Stick asked, still using his deep tone.

"Rose knows," Justin said, turning to the sweet-faced girl sitting cross-legged beside him.

Since none of the other children raised their hands, Andy called on her to answer.

"God gave us the gift of Jesus, so we give gifts to one another."

"Right on," Stick said, giving her a thumbs-up and temporarily slipping out of his wise-man mode. "That is . . . you're exactly right. Now, since God loved us so much that He sent Jesus into the world to show us how to love one another, we have some gifts for you."

Getting to his feet, he hoisted his robes and

moved—very carefully—toward the Christmas tree. As he called out names, Stephanie snapped Polaroid pictures of the children receiving their gifts.

Ruthie's vision blurred with tears. If Sean could only see this. Maybe if he could witness his friend in this role, he'd be less likely to judge Stick for trying to tend to his business.

After a closing song and a prayer, Justin ran up to Ruthie. "Can I get my picture took with the wise man?"

"He's not a real wise man, Justin."

"I know that. But I got my picture took with Santa Claus. Don'tcha think this is a lot better?"

"Well, yes," she had to agree. "But you'll have to ask Stephanie." The last thing Ruthie needed right now was for Sean to think she'd schemed to get a picture of Stick—in or out of a costume!

By the time Stick got out of his royal robes and beat it toward home on his trusty ol' bike, it was late. Mom would have already left for the night shift, and Grandpa would be alone in the trailer.

That wouldn't be so bad, except that lately Stick had been worried about the old man. He hadn't been his usual cheerful self, joking around—at least, the best he could with his funny, slurred speech. His tremors were worse, and he'd seemed to be getting stiffer, more like a robot out of control.

The doctor had increased his medication, which had helped some. But Grandpa wasn't in good shape, no matter how you looked at it. Not only that, but his extra medicine took about all they had left after paying bills. Maybe he ought to ask Sean about getting a little part-time job at the supermarket warehouse. That would be *one* way of seeing his ol' buddy more often.

He pedaled faster, hunching his shoulders against the raw wind. It wasn't good for Grandpa to be by himself too long. . . .

Overnight, a light snowfall had iced the entire area like a giant birthday cake. Most of the snow had melted during the day, except for patches that had refrozen when the sun went down.

On the bridge, Stick hit an icy spot and skidded crazily but managed to right himself before pitching headfirst over the handlebars. Whew! Close call.

Heart still thudding, he turned down the lane and rode up to the trailer. After propping his bike against the side, he hurried in out of the cold, rubbing his hands together inside his gloves.

But the sound that greeted him froze the blood in his veins. Grandpa was calling for help! But where was he?

A quick check revealed that he was not in his wheelchair in the front room. Nor was he in bed, where Stick had expected to find him tucked in all nice and cozy.

He was in the bathroom, sprawled on the floor like a marionette tangled in its strings. *Must have tried to get up by himself, and I wasn't here to help him!* Stick groaned inwardly.

"That you . . . Aric? Help . . . me. . . ."

Eleven

"Great party," Natalie commented on the way home. She glanced over her shoulder at Justin, playing with his new toy in the backseat. "The kids had a ball, and the single moms and dads seemed to enjoy it just as much."

Ruthie kept her eyes on the road, steering carefully over the patchy snow. "Yeah. Wonder what happened to their marriages. Most of them are divorced, you know."

"Maybe they got married for the wrong reasons. My mom and dad have always said love isn't enough. They say a marriage that isn't built on faith in God won't work."

Everyone knew the Ainsworths were crazy in love with each other. Natalie sometimes even mentioned that it was downright embarrassing how they carried on like two teenagers. But Mr. and Mrs. A., who were both Christians, had one of the best marriages around. "Guess we're the lucky ones," Ruthie told her friend. "You and I come from Christian homes where our parents care about each other. But not everyone is so lucky."

"You're talking about Sean," Natalie guessed.

Ruthie sighed. "Uh-huh. It must be hard not having a mom and a dad living in the same house."

"*Stick* doesn't have a dad," Natalie reminded her. "He's been dead for years."

"No, but he has his grandfather living with him." She couldn't help chuckling. "Stick doesn't even have a *car*."

"So if you don't have a dad and you don't have a car, you might grow up to be like Stick?" Justin piped up from the backseat. "Cool!"

Ruthie jerked her head around. "You been listening to our conversation, Pipsqueak?"

"No, you just talk so loud I couldn't hear myself think."

Natalie covered her mouth to restrain a giggle, and Ruthie groaned. She'd have to be more careful what she said in front of Justin. "Little pitchers have big ears," she said in an undertone, glancing over at Nat. Then, more loudly, "Sean's problems aren't necessarily because he doesn't have a father at home, Justin. Stick's doing just fine."

"Yeah, and he was the wise man tonight, too. I saw his tennis shoes sticking out from under his dress." He waited for the hoots of laughter to subside. "He knows all about Baby Jesus and where He's 'sposed to be at Christmas. That's more than *some* people know." He poked Natalie on the shoulder.

"Oh, Justin, don't you remember? We're waiting until Christmas morning to put Baby Jesus in the manger," Natalie assured him.

Justin mumbled something under his breath as

Ruthie pulled into her driveway and parked. He didn't wait until she'd turned off the ignition before he jumped out of the car and ran for the front door.

"We'll have to padlock my room if we want to get any talking done tonight," Ruthie said, switching off the engine and opening the door. "That boy never listens unless it's something you don't want him to hear!"

Natalie's laugh rang out as she stepped out of the car and followed Ruthie up the sidewalk. Their breath plumed like talk balloons in the frosty air.

"Justin will tell you all about the party, Mom," Ruthie told her mother once they were inside. "Nat and I have some things to discuss."

"Secrets again?" Maureen Ryan asked, cocking her head.

"No fair asking questions at Christmastime. Isn't that what you always tell me?"

"Oh, when I was your age, my friends and I talked about *boys*."

"Mo-om."

"Oh, go on with you, and discuss my present." She swatted at Ruthie with her dishtowel, giving Natalie a wink. "And if you need to know any sizes, I'll be happy to oblige. Come on now, Justin, and tell me what happened tonight at the church."

Seizing the moment to escape, Ruthie shot her mother a grateful grin and hurried down the hallway to her room. Inside, she bolted the door and leaned against it. "I was serious about the padlock," she told Nat. "Justin's been such a pest lately. And no one—do you hear me, Natalie Ainsworth?—*no one* must know what I'm about to tell you."

Natalie plopped down on the bed. "Okay, just what *did* you get your mom for Christmas?"

"Cute, Nat," Ruthie said, pulling off her shoes and curling up on the bed beside her friend. She started off with the romantic evening at Crystal's. "Sean was so sweet—most of the time—like he used to be before things got so bad for him at home."

She glanced at Natalie and tried to keep her voice steady. "It sort of made me wonder what it might be like to . . . you know . . . spend the rest of my life with him." Seeing Nat's mouth open in surprise, she quickly added, "You ever consider marrying Scott?"

"Well, yes. But that's light-years away. We both have careers to think about, even if I don't have a clue as to what mine will be."

"If I remember correctly, you were telling me that you don't want to date anyone but Scott. Now think this one over: What if he gave you a ring for Christmas and asked you to marry him and go to New York with him?"

Natalie shrugged it off. "It's not going to happen, Ruthie."

"I know. But, just suppose."

"I'd say no. He's just started a new career in modeling, and there's no telling where that will take him. Besides, I can't picture myself married. I'm just not ready for that kind of responsibility. And we really don't know each other all that well. I think we're both still growing in a lot of ways."

"What if Scott threatened to break up if you didn't become engaged?"

Natalie turned in surprise. "Did Sean do that?"

"No, he didn't." Sean may not have said the words, but Ruthie knew that's exactly what he'd do if she didn't keep his ring. It would be the end of their relationship. "You're not answering my question, Nat."

Natalie sighed. "Ruthie, I'm learning that my pat answers aren't always the best ones. Just like this "going-steady" thing. I *thought* I knew what I'd do, but that was before I started going out with Scott." She stared off into space, deep in thought. "I might go steady, but I would *not* become engaged. I hate the prospect of Scott finding another girl, of course, but that's a risk I'll just have to take. I know he's going to be tempted by those beautiful models. You should have seen the fuss they made over him in New York."

"Yeah, I can imagine," Ruthie sighed. "All the girls here think he's the greatest."

"See what I mean? So he's probably going to forget all about me when his career takes off. I think he knows it, too. That's why he said we should promise to meet *after* we finish college. In a way, although it sounds like he wants to hold on to me, I think it's a way of letting me go . . . gently."

Ruthie took time to absorb what she'd just heard. "But he didn't want all those other gorgeous girls, Nat. Katlyn was after him, too, remember? But he chose *you*. He wants a nice, steady Christian girl."

Natalie wrinkled her nose. "Maybe. I'll admit he needed me this past year, when he was really down. But his family troubles have smoothed out, and he's launching into a great new career. This will be the *real* test."

Natalie always made so much sense, Ruthie

thought, but she could tell her friend was hurting a little. Nat finally understood what it was like to be in love, afraid of what might happen out there in the future. Ruthie's heart went out to her. *But what kind of friend have I been to Sean when he needed me? I'm not a thing like Natalie. My temper flares up, and I speak my mind, pretty much like Sean does. We're like a couple of time bombs set to go off!*

"Okay, so what did Sean give you for Christmas?" Natalie asked, breaking Ruthie's reverie.

"Isn't a poinsettia and dinner at Crystal's enough for any girl?" Ruthie answered evasively, wondering if she should tell Nat the news after all.

"Sure, it's great." Natalie eyed the pink poinsettia on the nightstand, still fresh and beautiful. "Just like dinner at The View."

"So . . . did Scott give you your present?"

Natalie shook her head. "He's waiting till Christmas Eve." She let out a little giggle. "And he said it *has* to snow. Oh, Ruthie"—she picked up a toss pillow and hugged it to her—"that night on top of the Empire State building must mean as much to him as it does to me."

Ruthie was really happy for Nat. At the same time, she felt a big empty space, like a chasm opening before her. In a way, she was losing her best friend. Was she going to lose Sean, too?

"Okay," she said, suddenly decisive. She got up to stand in front of Natalie. "Close your eyes."

When Nat scrunched her eyes shut, Ruthie pulled the chain from beneath her sweater. "You can open up now."

Natalie blinked, looked bewildered, then glanced at the chain, now visible against Ruthie's navy sweater. There was the familiar little white dove. And the ring!

Ruthie watched her friend's hand move toward the diamond as if in slow motion. "That's not . . . what it looks like, is it?" Nat gasped. "Are you. . . ? Did you. . . ? Oh, Ruthie, is this for real?"

Ruthie lowered her voice to a whisper. "Sean asked me to marry him."

"What . . . what did you say?"

"I said I'd think about it."

Natalie stared at her for what seemed like an eternity. "What *I* think is that you'd better do some big-time praying. . . ."

Long after Natalie had left, Ruthie lay in bed, staring into the darkness. For once, Nat hadn't offered to pray with her. "*You're on your own this time, Ruthie,*" she'd said. "*You and God.*"

Hearing the cold wind howling outside her window, their old house creaking and groaning, and her own thoughts swirling around in her head like the flakes in Natalie's snow dome, Ruthie couldn't sleep. Finally, in desperation, she propped herself up, turned on the bedside lamp, and reached for her Bible. She flipped it open to Proverbs—the book of wisdom. She could use some of that right now. The words on the page sizzled to life as she read: *Trust in the Lord with all your heart and lean not on your own understanding; in all your ways acknowledge Him and he will make your paths straight.*

Letting the truth of those words wash over her like a warm bath, Ruthie picked up her diary. Lately, she'd been using it not just as a place to record personal stuff—her battle with weight, her struggles with Sean—but as a prayer journal. *Lord, I believe those words in the Bible,* she wrote. *It's not you I doubt. It's myself. Show me what to do. If I turn Sean down, he's going to need you more than ever. Even though I don't think he's given his heart to you, please don't leave him now. . . .*

The next thing Ruthie knew, her mom was knocking on the door. "You up, hon? It's Natalie . . . on the phone."

Springing out of bed, Ruthie rushed to the kitchen. Maybe Nat had had a vision in the night and would tell her what to do about Sean.

She stopped long enough to take a sip from the glass of orange juice her mom handed her. After seeing those poor little kids last night with only one parent— many of them moms who had no choice but to work long hours—Ruthie appreciated more than ever the fact that her own mother had chosen not to work Saturdays at the beauty shop. It was neat having her home. Suddenly, the idea of getting married and giving up her childhood home didn't look so great.

"Hi," she spoke into the phone, over the lump in her throat.

"Ruthie!" Natalie squealed. "Cissy just called to tell me Scott will be home this afternoon, and Antonio's with him! So Cissy's throwing a party for them tomorrow night after church. She said be sure to ask you and Sean."

"Sorry, Nat." Ruthie's heart took a nose-dive. "Sean's working tomorrow night, remember?"

"Well, get him to take some time off or switch hours with someone. Or . . . I don't suppose you'd come without him, would you? It's a drop-in anyway, and you could come and go whenever you wanted."

The idea was appealing. "Uh . . . I'll see," Ruthie hedged.

She'd barely hung up the phone when it rang again. This time it was Sean, sounding really upbeat. "I told Mom, Ruthie . . . about us. She's thrilled. Thinks you're the greatest. She even said we could live with her if we need to!"

Ruthie's thoughts screeched to a halt. *Live with Sean's mom? Move away from home? From her parents and Justin? From Natalie? And Sean would have to work day and night to make ends meet. She'd never see him!*

"Ruthie? You there?"

"Uh . . . yeah, Sean. I'm here."

"Have you told your mom and dad?"

"Not yet." She looked around, and seeing she was alone in the kitchen, she said, "Sean, we've got to talk." Hoping to stall a little longer, she changed the subject. "We're invited to a party tomorrow night—at Cissy's. Think you could get off work?"

"Come on, Ruthie. I'm not part of that crowd. And if you'd wake up and smell the coffee, you'd see you're not, either. It takes more than a fancy haircut and getting skinny to be in with *them*. Anyway, I couldn't get off work if my grandmother died! This is our busy season."

There was a long pause while Ruthie swallowed her

disappointment. Then Sean went on, "Look, if we're going to spend our lives together, we don't need those high-class dudes anyway."

Ruthie bit back a retort, feeling like a weight had settled on her chest.

"You won't go without me, will you?" Sean's voice was kind of whiny, like Justin's when he wanted something.

She sighed. "I guess . . . if we're going to spend our lives together, then we should go places together."

"That's my girl," he said, obviously relieved. "I know it hurts to have your best friend leave you for the fast lane. It's the same with my parents. They don't even speak to me these days unless it's to complain about the other one. The only civil conversation we've had in months is when I told Mom about us being engaged."

Ruthie allowed her mind to wander. A June wedding *would* be romantic. But *after* the wedding. . . ? "Sean," she began, trying for a reasonable tone of voice, "can we *afford* to do this? I thought you had money problems right now."

"Oh, that's all changed, Ruthie," he put in confidently. "I've found a way to make some extra money— lots of it!"

Sean held his breath for a moment after he hung up after his conversation with Ruthie, then let it out in a whoosh. No way could he tell her the complete truth. She'd never go along with it. Oh, he'd thought of telling her just enough about his new once-a-week delivery job, making more money than he made in an entire week at his regular job at the warehouse. But she'd ask too many questions. She'd want to know who'd pay that kind of money—and for what?

No, it was too risky. Besides, he wasn't going to keep his second job much longer anyway. Just long enough to put a little away to get married and buy them a decent car. Just a little longer. . . .

Twelve

The buzz at Sunday school the next morning was all about Stick's grandfather.

"Did you hear that he was found bound and gagged in his trailer when Stick got home from the single parents' party?" Twila whispered to Lana just before they gathered for the opening prayer.

"Isn't it awful what happened to Stick's Grandpa? He was beaten up and robbed last night!" Lana repeated to Amy Ainsworth.

By the time Ruthie got wind of the news, it was reported that both Stick and his grandfather had been held at gunpoint while two robbers ransacked the place and carried off a TV set, an heirloom pocketwatch, and Stick's baseball card collection!

Stick himself laid that rumor to rest by showing up about halfway through the opening assembly and giving them the real scoop. "Grandpa tried to get up by himself last night . . . and fell and broke his hip. He's in the hospital in a lot of pain, but they're giving him something for it. Mom will stay with him around the clock until he comes home in a few days."

Stick blushed the color of a ripe tomato. "Wouldn't

have happened if I'd been home when I said I would."

Ruthie and the others gathered around to console him. "You couldn't help it if the party ran longer than expected."

"That's right, Stick," Andy spoke up. "You did us all a favor by playing the part of the wise man last night. I'm just sorry your grandfather had to suffer because of it."

He turned a frown on the group. "As for some of the rest of you, this is a good example of what happens when a rumor spreads out of control. You've heard us say many times in here that God hates gossip. So don't pass on anything if you don't have your facts straight—or without the permission of the concerned parties. Now, let's pray for Mr. Gordon. . . ."

Just before they bowed their heads, Ruthie caught Natalie's eye and touched the ring under her blouse in a silent, desperate appeal. *Don't you dare breathe a word about this!* she mouthed.

She sure hoped Nat got the message, or this group would have her married and expecting triplets by sundown!

At cantata practice, Ruthie's voice was on key, but her heart was out of tune, and it showed in the music she was trying to sing.

"Hope you're not coming down with something," the choir director said with concern when she choked for the second time. After practice, he advised her to go home and get some rest.

She'd intended to do just that, but on the way

home, she remembered Cissy's drop-in. Sean had said the two of them didn't belong to that "high-falutin' " crowd. So what had happened to the old Ruthie Ryan—the one who could stand her ground with the best of them? And why was she taking orders from Sean? They weren't even married yet!

At home, her mom was all for it. "You didn't get out the whole time Natalie was in New York. Now with Sean working evenings . . . Just go on and have a good time, hon."

Ruthie changed into her best black dress, heels, and gold jewelry, then took a look at herself in the full-length mirror on the back of the bathroom door. She'd quit starving herself, but she thought she looked thinner anyway. Wouldn't this be a great time to show off her classy hairdo . . . and her ring? But of course that crowd wouldn't be impressed with a diamond the size of a bird's eye!

Not only that, but she remembered something Cissy had said—that if she'd married Ron when she was a senior, as she'd planned before the tornado touched down in Garden City, she'd have made the biggest mistake of her life. *If I keep Sean's ring, will I be making a mistake, too?*

Putting that dismal thought aside, Ruthie pulled into Cissy's spacious drive. She'd driven by the house with Natalie a few times but had never been inside. She almost backed right out when she saw the fancy cars lined up in front of the Georgian mansion in the most exclusive section of Garden City.

On second thought, Cissy had invited her, and she was determined to go—with or without Sean. The tiny lights on a massive tree in a front window winked a friendly welcome, and the uniformed woman at the door smiled and asked her in. This would be the housekeeper Natalie had told her about.

Glancing around the entry hall, Ruthie glimpsed the elegant living room where the Christmas tree sparkled in all its gold-and-white glory. Garlands of greenery trimmed in burgundy velvet bows wound around the stair railing, stretching all the way to a balcony above.

Hearing laughter down the hall, Ruthie felt a little apprehensive. But in the dining room, where a feast fit for a king was spread out on a banquet-sized table, Cissy spotted her right away.

"Ruthie, I almost didn't recognize you! I love your hair. *Where* did you get that cut?"

In the old days, Ruthie would have considered that a snide remark. The women in this family probably went to Chicago to have their hair done by some world-famous stylist. But things were different now. Cissy was Natalie's friend, and a friend of Natalie's. . . . "Actually, my mom cut my hair in our living room," she admitted with a little laugh.

"Wow! I didn't know she could do that."

"She's new at being a beautician, but she hopes to have her own shop someday."

Cissy smiled, and when Cissy smiled, the sun came out. "It makes you look . . . so mature."

"Thanks." Next thing Ruthie knew, she was being introduced to some of Cissy's other friends. Just as Ruthie was wondering what she could possibly say to these people, Cissy broke in, "I'll tell Nat you're here.

Help yourself to the goodies."

Ruthie noticed that the others appeared friendlier after the introductions. One of the girls, wearing cashmere and pearls, even commented that her new "do" was "stunning."

Ruthie reached for a china plate. *A far cry from chips and dip or Pizza Supreme at the Pizza Palace*, she thought, placing a few choice morsels on her plate. She would *not* eat like a pig, nor did she want to drop anything on the fine rug and disgrace herself.

At the end of the table, she picked up a fork. *Who cares if their forks are sterling silver and ours are stainless steel? Both kinds serve the same purpose.*

"What are you grinning about?" she heard as she turned to find Natalie standing behind her.

"Wouldn't do to say," Ruthie replied smugly.

"You look great. Amazing, how a haircut can change a person's looks."

"Same to you, friend. You're looking pretty spiffy yourself."

Natalie had on a dress Ruthie had never seen—probably one she'd bought with Cissy in New York—a white knit mini. She was wearing chunky heels and had brushed her hair in that style Ruthie liked—with one side pulled back and the other swinging forward over her face.

"Let's go get you something to drink, then I want you to come see Scott and meet Antonio."

"I really don't care about the refreshments," Ruthie said, lowering her voice. "I just wanted to see how the other half lives."

Natalie laughed. "I doubt if more than a favored

few live like this. But it really isn't important, you know."

"I know," Ruthie said, dropping her gaze to the little white dove resting on a gold chain around Nat's neck. This was one girl who never seemed to forget what was top priority, and she didn't mind advertising it.

She followed Natalie into a huge family room, only a little less formal than the living room. This one was paneled in rich, dark woods, with heavy brocade draperies and oodles of family portraits in gold frames. A roaring fire in the fireplace, flanked with dozens of poinsettias in shades of pink, red, and white, made you forget all about the icy weather outside. At a bar that separated this room from the kitchen, a maid was serving punch from a silver bowl.

Most of the young people were hanging around Scott and a guy Ruthie assumed to be Cissy's new boyfriend. She was positive that's who he was when Cissy walked up and he gave her a dazzling, mega-watt smile. Something was definitely going on here.

Just at that moment, Scott spied her coming in with Natalie. "Ruthie! How's it going? Where's Sean?" he asked, glancing around.

"He couldn't come. Work, you know." She shrugged, feeling guiltier than she should have. "Hey, congratulations on being discovered. It couldn't have happened to a nicer guy." When he only ducked his head modestly, she decided that he hadn't changed a bit. Still the same old Scott who had worked side by side with a clean-up crew after the tornado last spring. But he looked even better than she remembered. Lucky Nat.

"You need to meet Tony," he was saying, putting his hand on the guy's arm. "Antonio Carlo . . . Ruthie Ryan."

Antonio took her free hand and pressed it warmly. He was drop-dead gorgeous, with that olive skin and dreamy dark eyes. "When did you arrive?" he asked politely.

"Only a few minutes ago," Ruthie replied, puzzled.

"Then I'll tell you before anyone else does. My claim to fame is that I'm the klutz who hit Cissy over the eye with my camcorder and nearly destroyed her career!"

"Yes, and I've been keeping my distance ever since," Cissy said, laughing.

But it didn't look like "distance" to Ruthie. In fact, Cissy linked her arm through Antonio's and, still laughing, led him away to speak to some other guests.

Finally, Cissy spoke above the hum of conversation. "Okay, everyone, listen up. Now that we're all here, Scott and Antonio will take a few minutes to fill you in on the Big Apple—via the infamous videotape. So make yourselves comfortable and face toward the front. The show is ready to begin."

Ruthie and Natalie found a spot on one of the plush sofas and sank down—forever—into the cushions. As the lights lowered, a huge screen, recessed in the ceiling, dropped down to cover at least half the wall. "Wow!" Ruthie whispered to Nat. "The Bijou doesn't have anything on the Stileses."

For the next few minutes, they were treated to a mini-tour of New York City, including clips of the Macy's Thanksgiving Day Parade, interviews with some of the contestants in the Model Search, and finally, the actual pageant itself—with Cissy in the outfits she had modeled, ending with a knock-out wedding dress and a veil, skillfully arranged to cover her black eye. As she bowed her blond head, a taped recording of "The Lord's Prayer" brought tears to their eyes— and the New York audience to its feet.

As the winners were announced, Ruthie and Natalie were amazed all over again that Cissy hadn't won. "She was robbed!" Ruthie hissed to Natalie.

Afterward, when the lights came back up, Cissy stepped forward and took a deep breath.

Ruthie waited and watched. This was where she'd see the real Cissy—the one who had to win at any cost—the one who'd always had everything handed to her on a silver platter.

"I know you're all wondering how I felt after losing the competition," Cissy began. "To tell you the truth, I *wanted* to win. So it was pretty disappointing when I didn't."

Well, Ruthie thought, *that* was a surprise. She'd actually admitted she was *human*.

"I'm still trying to sift through all the reasons God would lead me to participate in a contest I couldn't win," Cissy went on. "While I still don't have all the answers, He has shown me a few of them. For one thing, I made a lot of new friends—some I hope to know better." Ruthie watched as Cissy glanced in Antonio's direction. His slow wink brought a rosy stain to Cissy's fair complexion.

"Another is that some of the girls we met had serious problems—and I learned just how blessed I am and how much I owe to others . . . and to God."

Ruthie noticed that some of Cissy's friends shifted nervously. Antonio, who had been standing to one side, moved silently toward the bar for a refill of his punch cup.

"I guess I just wanted to say thanks to those of you who prayed for me." Her eyes scanned the crowd, her gaze coming to rest on Natalie sitting beside Ruthie. "But it's God I want to thank most of all—not only for sending a tornado to turn me around the night I was eloping with Ron, but for giving me people like some of you to show me how to grow in Him. Contest or no contest, we're all winners when we choose Jesus."

The uncomfortable hush that settled over the room must be embarrassing for Cissy, Ruthie figured. But it was Scott who stepped in to ease the tension.

"That's not the end of the story, folks. What Cissy doesn't know—though she and Tony will kill me when they find out—is that I've put together a little footage to show you something really neat about a couple of terrific people. Hey, will someone get the lights again?"

This time, it was not a beautiful model flashing a set of perfect teeth who was smiling at the camera, but a grungy-looking little old lady with a buttonless coat and a snaggle-toothed grin. "This is Gertrude," Scott explained. "Nat and I met her the day of the parade. She was living in a New York alley." He waited for the groans of disgust to subside. "But it was Cissy—and Tony here—who really got the job done."

Even in the dim light, Ruthie could see Antonio's tanned skin take on a deep flush.

As the tape rolled, there were shots of Gertrude in

her cardboard "home"; Gertrude, with a mangy-looking little dog; Gertrude, still in her shabby coat, having Thanksgiving dinner in a fancy hotel.

"But here's the *real* happy ending." The next footage showed Gertrude at Macy's in a new bright red coat and cap, her arms loaded down with packages. "This is what Cissy did with her $500 gift certificate."

There were a few gasps from Cissy's rich friends. Even Ruthie's mouth dropped open. Nat hadn't told her about any of this. But then she hadn't had much of a chance to get a word in edgewise. Not with Ruthie dumping on her!

"And here's the clincher: Gertrude, in her new home—an efficiency apartment, rent-free, provided by none other than Antonio Carlo and family, owners of the Top Ten Modeling Agency!"

The final shot showed the happy little woman wearing a "Jesus Is the Reason for the Season" sweatshirt and sitting at a bright yellow kitchen table, loaded with grocery sacks.

When the lights came back up, Ruthie was ready to get out of there. What Cissy had done for that old lady was great, but it didn't make Ruthie feel any better. Now Cissy and Natalie were two of a kind—and three made a crowd.

So Ruthie was in total shock when Natalie asked for a ride home. "You're not going with Scott?"

"He picked me up, but I told him I'd ride home with you if you came. This is his party, too. Besides, he needed some time with his family."

On the way home, neither of them had much to say until Ruthie broke the silence. "Looks like Scott has his future all mapped out for him—either in front of the camera or behind it."

"Yeah." Nat was unusually glum. "That's what I've been trying to tell you. That's why I hope you and I will always be friends."

Ruthie shot her a puzzled glance. "But you have Cissy now, and all those other snobs—I mean, rich people."

"Oh, Cissy's wonderful, and I'm so glad she's found the Lord, but there's no one like you, Ruthie Ryan. Who else could keep me in stitches while we're struggling through junior college?"

There was another long silence. "I don't know if I'll be going to college, Nat. If Sean and I get married, I'll have to work, and Gertrude's paper shack will look like the Taj Mahal!" On the other hand, Sean had mentioned a second job—something that he expected to bring in lots of money. . . .

"So you've decided to go through with it."

Ruthie shrugged, keeping her eyes on the street ahead, still slick in spots.

"I noticed you weren't wearing your chain again— the one with your white dove and your ring. . . . The two just don't go together, do they?" Natalie asked softly.

"Well," Ruthie hedged, a little huffy at the implication, "not yet. But when we're ready to announce our engagement, I'll wear the ring—on my finger, where it belongs. That is, if Sean will wait for me to make up my mind," she mumbled under her breath.

"Look at it this way, Ruthie. What if Scott made some crazy demand—like having sex with him or giving up my college plans and marrying him right away—or else he'd run off with one of those New York models?"

Ruthie gave a short laugh. "I'd tell him to get lost!"

"Exactly. When we all took that vow of pure love, it wasn't just about sex or marriage or anything else. It was about putting others ahead of ourselves."

"*I* know that, Natalie. I go to the same church and took the same vow you did. We're supposed to want the best for the other person, even if we have to sacrifice our own desires . . . and that's what I'm willing to do . . . I think."

Natalie slanted Ruthie a sidelong look. "Yes, but it goes both ways. True love means the other person is willing to do the same for *you* . . . right?"

Ruthie didn't answer but drove on in silence, feeling more miserable by the second. When she pulled up in front of the Ainsworth house, Natalie turned in the seat to face her.

"Ruthie, I'm your best friend, remember? We've been best friends since we kicked the slats out of our cradles in the church nursery."

Ruthie had to smile at her friend's attempt at humor.

"You told me about you and Sean arguing a lot and how he'd left you stranded out in the cold at the church," Natalie went on. "I've even heard him get mad and call you some pretty unkind names a few times. But I don't think you're telling me everything. What's *really* bothering you?"

With that, the dam broke. The tears spilled out in a flood, along with the secret fear that Ruthie had barely admitted to herself. "Oh, Nat, I can't marry Sean!" she sobbed. "I don't know *where* he got the money for the ring and all the other stuff he's been doing for me lately, but it wasn't from that warehouse job!"

Thirteen

Ruthie was relieved when she didn't see or hear from Sean until Wednesday morning. She'd needed every bit of that time to think, pray, and be sure she was making the right decision. Now all she had to do was tell Sean.

"I've decided," she said over the phone when he called.

"Great! I'll pick you up tonight, and we'll make plans." His voice took on a sullen tone. "Guess you'll want to go to youth group first, though."

"It's the last meeting before Christmas, Sean. We give Stephanie and Andy their present tonight, so I really want to be there."

"Fine." He was his cheerful self again. "We'll stop by the Pizza Palace afterward and show off your ring to some of my buddies who hang out there sometimes. See you then."

The evening was cold and crisp, but the temperature had risen, and without the blustery wind, there was no chill factor. Sean came to the door wearing the sweater she'd given him for Christmas. Her heart lurched at the sight of him, looking so grown-up and handsome. He had already turned eighteen, had a steady job—two jobs, he'd said. And he loved her. What more could she want?

She'd loved him, too, for two years—more than an eighth of her whole life. A lot had happened in those two years.

There was a crowd in the youth lounge. Almost everyone had come tonight, Ruthie decided, glancing around. She didn't see Stick, though. He must be helping his mom with his grandfather—she'd heard they'd brought Mr. Gordon home today.

When Natalie called the meeting to order, Sean slouched in his chair, looking really bored . . . until she motioned Andy and Stephanie forward to receive their Christmas gift from the youth group—a gift certificate for dinner at Crystal's!

At that, Sean straightened and looked over at Ruthie. The look he gave her turned her knees to rubber. How could he still have that effect on her after all he'd put her through?

<hr />

When they pulled up into the rear parking lot of the Pizza Palace, Ruthie put her hand on Sean's arm. "Let's not go in yet. Let's talk out here."

She unclasped the chain around her neck, took off the ring, and handed it to him. "I can't accept this, Sean. I'm really flattered, but—"

He cut her off with a curse word she'd never heard any of her friends use. Even in the darkness, with only the neon lights of the restaurant flashing on his face, she could tell he'd turned pale. "Flattered!" He pushed her hand away. "We've been going together for two years—*two years*—and you said you loved me. Were you lying all that time?"

Her stomach gnawed, twisting and churning. "I do love you, Sean . . . that is, I *did*," she squeaked, feeling helpless. He couldn't possibly understand when she didn't understand herself. But something was wrong—something she couldn't put her finger on. "I guess I'm just not ready to settle down yet . . . or even to be engaged," she finished.

"So you can date someone else! That's it, isn't it?" He grabbed her wrist, twisting it. "You're bored because I work most nights, and you're craving excitement with those jet-set friends of yours!" His gray eyes were like cold steel.

"I do not, Sean Jacson! I *do not* crave excitement, and I *have not* dated anyone but you!" Now that she thought about it, going steady had been a pretty dumb idea. How could a person know how to choose the right mate without any basis for comparison?

Now she'd really made him mad, and she eased her free hand to the door handle in case she needed to jump out and make a run for it. Suddenly, everything came clear. What kind of life could she have living in fear that her husband was going to blow up any minute? His parents' trouble had infected him like a virus . . . and she wasn't licensed to practice medicine!

"Don't you trust me, Ruthie? Haven't I proven how hard I'll work to take care of you?"

"I . . . I'm not sure," she said honestly, keeping her

voice low and soothing. "I just know I'm not mature enough . . . to handle marriage."

He took a deep breath and released his grip on her wrist. She knew he was trying to control his temper. "It is kinda scary, isn't it?" he said conversationally. "I had a cousin in his thirties who got married, and he was nervous, too, even with a good-paying job, a great car, and an apartment. But we can make it, Ruthie. I know we can."

He smiled, and Ruthie caught a glimpse of the old, sweet, gentle Sean. "How about putting the ring on your finger and just let me see it for a couple of minutes? I promise I'll put it in my pocket when we go inside." He gave her that little-boy look that always melted her defenses.

For a minute, Ruthie was tempted. You couldn't just turn off love like a faucet—even if she didn't understand what was going on. If he wouldn't get so angry all the time, she might not ever want to take it off.

But we've been through all this. I've got to quit living this way—up one minute and down the next. One day eating like a pig because I'm tired of being insulted; the next, starving myself because he thinks I'm fat. I want to be me again. . . .

"I have a surprise, Ruthie," he said with that wonderful grin that used to make her heart go flip-flop. Right now, she dreaded hearing what he had to say. "I've told a few people . . . about us. Some of the guys at the warehouse. . . . I even called Andy."

Ruthie was shocked. "*Andy!* What did he say?"

"He tried to talk me out of it, but when he couldn't, he said they'd pray for us. I guess I've mentioned it to a few others—like Craig, when I ran into him at the mall." He flexed the muscle in his jaw. "But I haven't told your friend Natalie."

"Well, *I* did. She's my best friend, Sean. We tell each other everything."

"Yeah, that's just what I expected out of you." He was almost snarling. "You think more of her than you do of me!"

"At the moment, you better believe it!" Ruthie blurted out, too upset to worry about the consequences. "Am I supposed to choose between the two of you?"

Something glittered in his eyes, and Ruthie cringed. "Surely you wouldn't choose a girl over me," he said, daring her to admit it.

"Sean, she's my girlfriend, and you're my boyfriend. It's not the same. But this does tell me there's no use trying to make a go of our relationship." She took off the ring and held it out.

He slapped at her hand, sending the ring flying onto the dashboard. "So you're going to embarrass me in front of everybody, is that it?"

Don't argue with him, came a little voice, but she was too ticked off to listen. "Wouldn't it be much more embarrassing to announce an engagement and then have to tell everyone there's not going to be a wedding? Don't you see, Sean? All we do is fight."

His mood shifted again. "That's because it's so much fun making up. Come on, Ruthie. . . ."

She began to cry softly, and he tried to draw her into his arms, but she pushed him away.

Anger blazed in his eyes. "Don't do that," he warned in a lethal tone.

"Then get your hands off me," she said, crying harder.

"Come on, Ruthie, you're my girl. Let's make up."

She pushed him again, harder, and he fell back against his door. "I'm *not* your girl. *Cissy's* friends treat me better than you do!"

"You went to that party, didn't you? After I told you not to."

"You can't tell me what to do." She turned and grabbed the door handle just as she felt his hand on the collar of her jacket, yanking her backward. Choking, she turned her head just as he let go, drew back, and belted her on the mouth.

The door came open, and she stumbled out of the car and ran, holding her mouth and staring back at him in horror. He was peeling off the sweater she'd given him.

"Take this, too! I don't want anything to do with you! Ever!"

She gasped and jumped as the sweater came flying across the pavement and landed at her feet. She heard the door slam, and as she slumped to the ground, with her face against the cold brick wall, she felt the warm trickle of blood on her fingers. Her lip began to ache, and her head throbbed.

With her sobbing and the sound of Sean's car spinning out of the lot, she didn't hear the approaching footsteps until she felt someone's hand on her shoulder.

"Please . . . no!" she gasped, afraid that Sean had come back to finish her off.

"Take it easy," came a familiar voice. "It's only me."

Not *him* again!

"Don't worry, it'll be okay," Stick said, patting her arm as tenderly as a baby. "Let's see what that jerk did to you."

She waited, still sobbing, while Stick assessed the damage. "All I can see in this light is a few cuts, but you'll be plenty sore by tomorrow, I bet." Stick mopped at her face with a clean handkerchief he pulled out of the pocket of his jeans. "We'd better get you cleaned up and call someone to come get you. All I've got tonight is the Green Demon, and I don't think you're quite up to that." He gestured toward his bicycle, propped against the back of the building. "Anyone home at your place?"

"M-my mom." Ruthie hiccuped, touching her lip, which was beginning to swell.

"Come on. I'll help you inside, and we can call her. Don't worry," he said, noticing Ruthie's expression of alarm. "There's not much business right now . . . and you can count on me not to spread it around."

How had it come to this? Stick Gordon—coming to her rescue twice after Sean ran out on her. Stick was a good guy—a good friend. Thinking of the way she'd talked about him in the past, she burst into a fresh spasm of sobs.

Leaning on Stick's arm, Ruthie moved unsteadily toward the side entrance of the restaurant. Inside, there was only one other couple, too absorbed in each other to notice that anyone else was around.

While Stick used the pay phone to call her mom, Ruthie headed for the rest room on the other side of the takeout counter. Though she kept her head down, she didn't miss Phyllis Haney's raised eyebrows and questioning gaze. It followed her all the way to the swinging door.

———

Stick was hot with anger! If he ever caught up with Sean Jacson, he intended to give that jerk a piece of his mind—buddy or no buddy! Where did he get off treating Ruthie that way?

But what chance did a guy on a bike have against a guy in a car—even if it was an old clunker?

Once Ruthie was safely on her way home, Stick pedaled off toward the trailer, where he found his mom leaving for work.

He listened to her instructions about Grandpa, told her good-bye, then called Sean. Maybe he'd be home by now, and Stick could explain what he was doing at the Pizza Palace in the first place—just in time to see Sean making like a macho man. But after six rings, no one answered. He'd have to try again tomorrow.

Just then he heard Grandpa calling out from the bedroom. He'd been in terrible pain ever since they'd put that pin in his hip at the hospital, and the pain medication didn't hold him long enough. *"Now, Aric, don't you dare let him have another pill until eleven-thirty,"* Mom had warned. *"That stuff is terribly addictive."*

So what was the poor old guy supposed to do—suffer for another hour? Stick raced off to the bedroom. Maybe he could read to his grandpa or something.

———

It was late—real late—when Stick pedaled his bike

out to Little Egypt Supermarket Warehouse on Friday night. He'd given up trying to reach Sean on the phone, and now that school was out for the holidays, he wouldn't be seeing him in class. So catching him after hours at the warehouse was the last resort.

Good thing it was a clear night, too—no snow predicted until tomorrow, Christmas Eve!

The prospect of a white Christmas was the last thing on Stick's mind as he wheeled into the back lot of the huge warehouse complex. Looking around, he spotted Sean's old car parked near some trees a pretty good distance from the building with its bright floodlights.

Stick leaned his bike against a big oak near the fence and checked Sean's car door. It was unlocked. To keep warm while he waited, he climbed into the backseat.

For a few minutes, he watched the traffic coming and going as the shift changed. A steady stream of workers filed in and out of the building, but there was no sign of Sean. It shouldn't be long now, though.

He really needed to see Sean. Not only was there this thing with Ruthie, but with his grandfather needing extra medicine, Stick had to find a way to earn some money. He was hoping Sean could show him the ropes and help him get on here at the warehouse during the holidays.

A low-slung sports car rolled up beside Sean's car. In the near darkness, Stick couldn't make out the identity of the driver or the passenger sitting in the front seat.

When Sean finally appeared at the end of a line of

workers, Stick started to open his door and call to him. But seeing the two guys hop out and rush to meet him, Stick laid low.

"Did you bring the stuff?" he heard Sean ask before looking around to see if he'd been overheard. Spotting Stick in the backseat of his car, he ran over and jerked the door open. "What are *you* doing here, goofball?"

"I've been trying to get in touch with you for days, Sean." Stick unfolded his long legs and got out. "Don't you ever get your messages?"

"Yeah. It's *you* who hasn't gotten the message. I *don't* want to talk to *you*."

With the other two guys hanging back, Stick decided to put it all on the table. "Look, it's about Ruthie—and maybe getting a job here at the warehouse. We need the money for Grandpa's pain medicine."

There was a momentary flicker of sympathy in Sean's expression. "Sorry about your grandfather . . . but *Ruthie* is none of your business! Now bug off before you really make me mad!"

One of the other guys stepped up, and Stick recognized Bud, Phyllis Haney's brother. "You heard him, buddy. Get lost." Turning to Sean, he went on, "Security's going to be nosing around here. Do we have a deal . . . or not?"

The second guy put a hand on his arm. It was the older dude—the one with the thin mustache and the long cigarette. Stick had met him the same day he'd met Bud at the Pizza Palace.

"Wait up. We might just have ourselves a sweeter little deal than we thought." He squinted at Stick. "Say your granddad's sick, pal . . . having a lot of pain?"

Stick nodded, still not sure what was going on here.

"Well, if you can come up with the cash, I think we could find something to put him out of his misery."

Fourteen

It didn't take Stick long to figure out that he'd stumbled into something big. These guys weren't just dealing in small-time stuff—the kind Sean might be hooked on.

"We can get the old man whatever he needs—coke, crack, LSD, the works," said the smooth-talking guy—the one Stick remembered as Cliff. "And there's another drug that'll set him free. Ever hear of Dilaudid?"

"Yeah, I've heard of it." His mom knew all about drugs. Dilaudid was the most potent painkiller made—used mostly for cancer patients in a terminal stage. He wondered why the doctors hadn't prescribed it for Grandpa. Watching him suffer hour after hour was torture. . . . "I don't have the cash on me," Stick mumbled. "I'd have to—"

"Sure, sure, pal. We understand. We'll just finish our little deal with your buddy here, and you can think it over. If you decide to do business, we'll even cut him in . . . since he introduced us, ya know. Ha, ha!"

Stick watched with a sinking heart as they pulled out brown paper bags from their jacket pockets while Sean reached for his wallet and peeled off a few bills from a small roll. Never in a million years would Stick have thought he would be a witness to a drug deal, much less actually considering making one of his own. . . .

Shivering, Stick crammed his hands into the pockets of his jeans. Something hard struck his right hand— the extra set of keys to Grandpa's car . . . with the little white dove charm! He wasn't alone. He had the power of God on his side. Besides, if he went through with this, how would he ever live with himself? Not to mention Grandpa. He'd disown him! Feeling a surge of courage he didn't know he had, Stick drew himself up to his full height. "Hey, I've changed my mind. Deal's off. I'm outta here."

He was turning to head for his bike when he felt his arms pinned behind him. He was whirled around, and a hard jab to his jaw snapped his head back. The next punch to his middle doubled him over.

Leaving him gasping for breath on the ground, Cliff—with Bud close behind—jumped into the sports car, started the engine, and spun out, leaving a warning for Sean that barely registered in Stick's foggy brain. "Better tell your pal that he'll get worse than that if he squeals!"

Sean helped Stick to his feet, retrieved the bike while Stick leaned against the car, and stowed it in his trunk.

"Come on, big guy. Let's get you home." He eased Stick into the backseat again, as gently as possible. "Sorry you had to get involved. I wanted to spare you . . . but you had to butt in where you didn't belong."

Stick groaned as Sean ran around to the front seat and slid behind the wheel.

"I'll be . . . okay," Stick stammered between short breaths. "I've been elbowed, punched . . . and knocked down before."

"Yeah, but only on the basketball court."

Sean didn't hear any more from Stick for a minute or two. "Just take me home, okay? My mom will know what to do. And Sean . . ."

"Yeah, Stick?"

"Let's . . . finish that talk . . . tomorrow."

"Sure, buddy, sure." There was a long pause while Sean collected his thoughts. "Just don't rat on me, will ya?"

After the trailer door closed behind Stick, Sean transferred the brown paper bags from his pocket to the glove compartment of his car. Then he got in and leaned over to take out a pack of cigarettes. *If ever I needed one of those marijuana cigarettes I mixed in with the others—it's now!*

It was a scary thought. *No! I don't really need it.* He stuffed the pack in his pocket. What he needed was to get out of here, away from all reminders of what had just taken place in the warehouse parking lot. He put the key in the ignition, ground the engine, and tore out of the dirt lane, careening down the road.

I'm not hooked! I know better than that.

When he got home, he bypassed his mom and made for his room. He'd never felt sicker. Sick and tired and dirty . . . like he'd betrayed all his friends . . .

Ruthie, most of all. He'd been so mean to her. Well, he'd gone and done it now—ruined everything! He hated himself, hated his parents, his job, hated feeling guilty about the joints—selling 'em, using 'em. He'd done his best to avoid Stick, the straightest guy he knew. But now he'd probably ruined *his* chances, too. What college would want Stick now if they ever found out he'd been an eyewitness to a drug deal?

Sean shoved his hands in his jacket pocket, and his fingers closed over the pack of cigarettes. *One more.*

He walked over and locked his door, then opened his window, feeling a rush of cold air that cleared his head for a minute. "Just one more," he repeated as he struck a match to the tip of the cigarette.

A wry smile tugged at his lips as he lit up and drew the smoke into his lungs. Come to think of it, Stick had only gotten what he deserved. He'd had no business snooping around anyway. *I was in a tight spot, and I did something stupid*, Sean reasoned to himself. *Okay, so I won't do it anymore. But . . . I've got to get my money's worth for this last batch.* Then . . . no more!

As he continued to puff away, a little shiver went through him. Right now one person—and only one—controlled his entire future. Stick Gordon. Would Stick turn him in to the police? Would his ol' buddy have him arrested for pushing drugs? *But I'm not a real pusher. I've only done a favor for some of the guys at the warehouse a few times. It's not like standing outside a school yard, waiting for little kids.*

Oh, the boss had tried to reel him in—had told him there was plenty of big money if he'd supply a list of some of his friends at Shawnee High. But he hadn't gone that far. Stick owed him that much. So did a lot of other guys—if they only knew it.

He took another long draw and felt better about himself. After all, what he did was none of Stick's business. Or Ruthie's, for that matter. He was eighteen now—legal age. He could do as he pleased.

But just in case Stick decided to sic the authorities on him, he'd better be prepared. He ground out the stub and as soon as it was cool enough, stuffed it in the pack, put that in his pocket, left his room, and walked down the hall to the bathroom.

He locked the door and began to break the cigarettes in half and toss them into the commode. No point in smoking those. But there was one brown one left. He held it in his hand for a moment and grinned. "This is really the last one."

Already, he felt more relaxed. No need to stay awake all night wondering what his ol' buddy Stick was going to do. *Why waste a good night's sleep?* he thought as he reached into his pocket for a pack of matches.

The next morning, after having spent most of the night at the hospital, Stick lay on the couch, his chest bandaged under his open shirt. Good thing Mom had taken a leave of absence a while back to take care of Grandpa. Now she had *two* patients!

For the last hour, he'd been trying to reason with his grandfather, who seemed to be feeling more chipper than he had in a long time. Whatever they'd been giving him for pain must have kicked in.

"Don't worry about me, Grandpa. The doctor said

the cracked rib will heal in no time—" Stick touched his side gingerly and winced. "There was no internal bleeding—just a few bruises. I've had my share of those before."

"Yes, yes, Aric," Grandpa waved his hand in a spastic gesture. "Your mother says you'll be fine . . . and she should know. It's that boy I'm worried about. If he gets away with this . . . he'll just get into worse trouble. Now, do you want to be re-shponsible for that?"

Stick drew in a deep breath and grimaced. With effort, he sat up. "No, sir. But I don't want to see Sean thrown in jail, either. I don't see how that would help him any." *Besides, it could be me! If it hadn't been for that little dove. . . .*

The old man stared off through the window. For a minute, Stick was wondering if he'd lapsed into another one of his silent spells. Then he spoke, his speech slurred a little, but understandable. "Aric, do you know why I'm better? It's not the medicine . . . it's not even the good nursing. . . ." He gave a lopsided smile as Stick's mom came into the room. "It's the Word."

"The Word?"

Grandpa pulled a small, black Bible from the pocket of his robe. "*God's* Word. Remember when you read to me that night? Well, 'my strength . . . cometh from the Lord.' I've been quoting that ever shince . . . to myshelf." He smiled again. "Mush-mouth," he quipped, pointing shakily to his tongue.

"Been doing some praying, too," Grandpa went on, " 'bout your friend. And thish is what came to me lash night. . . ."

158

Following his grandpa's instructions, Stick had made a couple of phone calls. Andy and Stephanie arrived a few minutes before Sean.

Mom was way cool, not even flinching when she invited Sean in, and actually offering him hot chocolate and cookies, of all things!

Grandpa smiled, too, but Stick wasn't fooled. The old man wasn't about to dance around the truth. He could only guess what poor Sean had coming.

Andy got right to the heart of the matter as soon as they gathered around the small table, attached to the wall between the kitchen and living room. "Did you have drugs on you, Sean?"

Sean took a deep breath. Stick knew there was nothing he could do but admit it. Why else would you pay someone money for two brown paper bags? Sean nodded, looking pretty miserable.

"You know you could be in a lot of trouble legally, don't you?"

"I know. And I'm sorry. Sorry, too, that Stick got in the middle of it." Sean began to explain how he'd only wanted to make a little extra money to set aside for his future and had been buying marijuana and re-selling it to some of the guys. "In the warehouse, mostly."

"You on the stuff yourself, Sean?" Andy asked.

"No . . . uh, that is, I did try it a few times, but I know better than to get hooked on stuff like that." Looking really uncomfortable, he pushed the chair back and braced his hands on the table, ready to bolt. "I don't have to answer all these questions."

But Grandpa halted him on his way up. "You're

wrong, boy. It's either us . . . or the police."

Sean dropped his eyes and settled back into his chair.

"Do you think this is the way God wants you to live your life?"

Sean's lips twitched, then something hard and metallic glinted in his eyes. "Yeah. God wants me to break my back at that warehouse, and still not be able to pay the rent, so Mom will have to go on welfare. He wants me to fail my senior year so I can never get a decent job. He wants me to love my dad, who hits my mom and will never be anything but a grease monkey."

"Well, Sean," Grandpa drawled, "so you'd rather be a drug-pusher?"

No one said anything for a long moment.

"You're eighteen now, aren't you?" Andy spoke up. At Sean's nod, he went on, "Did you stop to think that if you were caught, you could be tried in court as an adult?"

Sean shook his head. "Guess I didn't see it as a crime."

Grandpa gave Sean as level a look as he could manage. "What about the two young men who beat up my Aric? That's a crime . . . assault, I think they call it . . . and you didn't do anything to shtop it."

Stick had never seen Sean look so scared. "You going to have me arrested?"

You could have heard a feather drop. Stick finally broke the long silence. "No way, buddy. It's okay. We just want to help."

"Your whole life is ahead of you, Sean," Stephanie said. "I'm just sorry you didn't feel you could come to us."

Sean shrugged. "There's nothing you guys—or anyone else—could do. My life is one big mess . . . it's hopeless."

Stick saw the twinkle in Grandpa's eyes. "Hopelesh? No such thing, boy. Not if you have the Lord to lean on."

That was just the trouble, Stick thought, sure Sean would take off now. Sean *didn't* have the Lord in his heart—at least, as far as Stick knew. And that's where he had let his buddy down. Well, he wouldn't let him down again. They were going to have that talk he'd been promising.

"Now that you know the Gordons aren't going to press charges, what about cutting off your drug connections?" Andy asked, getting down to practical matters.

Sean shifted nervously. "I don't know. I know I can't go back to work on the night I'm supposed to get my next batch. They'd work me over worse than Stick."

"You could get another job. Hasn't your dad been needing an assistant?"

From that look in his eye, Sean was getting ready to be stubborn again, Stick figured. That is, until Grandpa spoke up. "Look at it thish way, Sean. I don't want to threaten you, but if I hear of you having anything to do with drugs again . . . you'll have a jail sentence slapped on you before you know what hit you. Understand?"

Sean swallowed hard, studying the shaky man who'd never looked stronger in his life to Stick. *It's what's on the* inside *that counts*, Stick thought.

Sean dropped his head. "Yes . . . sir. And . . . thanks for giving me another chance."

Feeling a weight roll off his shoulders, Sean left the trailer and headed for his dad's apartment. It was the last place on earth he wanted to go—except for jail, of course—but he really didn't have a choice.

His old man was a loser, and Sean was afraid he was following in his footsteps. He'd seen too much at home from his folks—yelling, fighting, cursing each other out. . . . But he hadn't done much better. He'd probably lost his best friend forever—no matter what Stick said—and he doubted if Ruthie would ever speak to him again—especially now.

His dad was puttering around with an old car in the apartment garage when he showed up. "Dad?"

His head snapped up, and a surprised grin spread across his face when he saw Sean. He reached for a rag to wipe his greasy hands.

"About that ad you put in the paper . . ."

Fifteen

Christmas Eve—the time of year when dreams come true—right?

The swelling in Ruthie's mouth had gone down, and she was able to move her lips without pain. But she still wasn't sure she'd be able to sing her solo tomorrow night. How could she hit those high notes when her heart had sunk to an all-time low?

"I really don't feel like company," Ruthie said when Natalie called that afternoon and wanted to come over. "I told Mom a little of what's been going on, and it's like she couldn't believe I'd keep something that important from her. She'll probably never speak to me again."

"Oh, Ruthie, you know that's not true."

"I don't know much of anything anymore."

"Well, I'm coming over anyway. I really have to talk to you. Stephanie and I will be there as soon as I pick her up."

At that, Ruthie moved the receiver to arm's length and stared in disbelief. Somewhere in the distance, she could hear Nat saying, "Ruthie, are you still there? Say something." Ruthie hung up.

Ruthie knew she was being difficult. But even her best friend couldn't help her now. And why did Stephanie have to come? What did she have to do with anything?

A horrible thought dawned. Sean! Something's happened to Sean!

Ruthie and her whole family were waiting in the living room when Natalie and Stephanie arrived. "Andy thought . . . I should be the one to tell you, Ruthie," Natalie began.

"Tell me what?"

As the whole ugly story spilled out—the drug dealers, their attack on Stick, Sean's using and selling— Ruthie felt she would die. "I can't believe this! It's a nightmare! But it does add up—Sean's mood swings, his fits of anger . . . all those things we've learned about drugs in youth group. I even suspected he was smoking, but I never thought it was anything like marijuana. I feel like I'm to blame, you guys! I should have—"

"Don't beat yourself over the head about this, Ruthie," Stephanie said in a consoling tone. "Sean's an adult now. He's responsible for his own actions, and he's promised never to do drugs again. Stick's rib will heal, too, so the Gordons aren't going to press charges. But Stick might like to see some friendly faces right about now."

Ruthie took a deep breath. "Yeah. I'm afraid I haven't been a very good friend to Stick. In fact," she said with chagrin, "I've given him a pretty hard time. I definitely want to apologize—especially since it was my boyfriend who caused him so much trouble."

"What about now?" Nat asked. "Christmas Eve seems the perfect time . . . and Stephanie knows the way to Stick's place."

Ruthie was getting her jacket out of the coat closet when she heard Justin's little voice. "I felt like something awful was going to happen," he piped up. "I knew it. I just knew it."

In the car with Nat and Stephanie, Ruthie blurted out what was on her mind. "Can you believe it?" she said. "I was part of the youth group single parents' party, when we tried to bring some Yuletide cheer to all those kids. But I can't even help my own brother. I'm depressing a little guy who's never had a worry in the world!"

The three of them piled out of the car when they reached the trailer. When she'd heard that Stick lived in a mobile home, Ruthie had thought "Trailer Park," but this wasn't bad at all. Perched on a hill, the white trailer with its dark green shutters looked really nice. She turned to look down the long dirt road, flanked by an impressive stand of tall trees. "I'll bet this place is gorgeous in the summertime."

"Or with snow on those evergreens," Natalie said wistfully.

"You've had snow on the brain ever since that New York trip," Ruthie quipped to hide her nervousness. She hadn't a clue as to what she was going to say to Stick.

Stephanie rang the doorbell. A tall woman with

short, dark curls opened the door and greeted them. Stick's mom, no doubt. She had the sweetest face and huge, dark eyes like his.

The moment they stepped inside, Ruthie detected the aroma of pine needles and spiced apple cider—a homey smell. The living room was small, so in one sweeping glance, she took in the couch where Stick lay all bandaged up, a couple of easy chairs, and a wheelchair occupied by a gray-haired man, who sat slightly hunched forward. This must be Stick's grandfather.

Stick did his best to bound off the sofa to greet the guests, but he only succeeded in bumping his head on the low ceiling. "Ouch!" he said, rubbing the short bristles on top of his head with one hand and clutching his bandaged side with the other. "I keep forgetting."

He made the introductions, and when he came to his grandfather, the old man lifted a shaky hand. Natalie and Stephanie shook briefly, then Ruthie stepped up and grasped his hand in both of hers.

"Been wanting to meet you," he said. She could understand perfectly, even though his speech was slow and slurred.

"I've been wanting to meet you, too, Mr. Gordon," she said, still holding his hand. "I'm so sorry about—"

"Don't have to say it," he replied. "You being here says it all. Actions, you know—" he managed to wink—"louder than words."

Ruthie felt a tingle of warmth flow from his hand all the way up her arm. Afraid he might be offended by her scrutiny, she carefully let go and looked over at the table, where Mrs. Gordon had brought cups of hot cider and a plate of chocolate chip cookies.

A scrawny pine stood in the corner, with colored lights and strings of popcorn. There were some home-made ornaments—some of them obviously dating back to the days when Stick was a little guy.

"We don't have room for a very big tree," Mrs. Gordon said, following Ruthie's glance. "But ever since Aric was a little boy, he and I have added another ornament each year. We still do." She smiled sweetly. "This year, the ornament was a wise man."

Stick grinned his silly grin and turned red, but he didn't reprimand his mom for telling.

"Now, the popcorn is a different matter. Aric . . . eats more of it than . . . he strings." Funny how Ruthie could pick up on every word Mr. Gordon said, even though it was difficult for him to speak.

"Well," Stick went on, "I've never eaten an orna-ment."

"No? What happened to the candy canes?"

"Those aren't ornaments."

"Matter of def-inishun . . . wouldn't you say, Miss Ruthie? I hear you're good . . . in English."

Ruthie was surprised. Now where had he heard a thing like that? Why should Stick discuss her with his grandfather? Maybe Andy or Stephanie had said some-thing on one of their visits. From somewhere, a coher-ent thought formed. "I'm nowhere when it comes to science and math, but I suppose English *is* my best subject, Mr.—"

There was a strange gurgling sound before the next words came out. "Don't call me . . . 'Mister.' I'm just . . . Grandpa."

"Grandpa," Ruthie echoed.

His smile didn't quite settle in the right place, but Ruthie couldn't take her eyes from his. They were the warmest, kindest eyes she'd ever seen. They seemed to know so much, and it was a shame he couldn't tell it all with his mouth. When he nodded, she was sure it was intentional and not one of those uncontrollable movements that happened sometimes. But Ruthie felt an uncontrollable urge to get on with her apology to Stick, and she was relieved when the others moved to the couch and chairs and left the two of them at the little table, with Grandpa nearby in his wheelchair within hearing distance.

"Even when Sean ran out on me those times, I didn't want him to feel I was running out on *him*," Ruthie tried to explain to both of them. "But . . . well . . . I've been so upset, I haven't been able to think straight."

Stick was staring down at his hands. Then suddenly he looked up, right into her eyes. "I don't have any answers about Sean, either. But you mustn't let anyone— or anything—stand in the way of using all the gifts God has given you, Ruthie."

"Gifts?" she questioned, wondering if he was going to make some kind of joke since it was so near Christmas.

He nodded, gazing at her with big, serious eyes. "For one thing, you're good at singing."

Ruthie remembered claiming to have a sore throat at cantata practice. Actually, her throat had closed up because of all the stress with Sean. "I can't sing when I'm upset."

"I know how you feel, Ruthie," Stick said. "My dad

died when I was five years old. It was no comfort to me that everyone said he was in heaven. I wanted him *here*. I'd cry myself to sleep every night. But during the day, Grandpa here made me do things. He'd say, 'Do it for your dad and for the Lord,' but I didn't see how that was going to bring my dad back. I'd get so mad I'd slam that basketball on the ground, or toward the net. I took my anger out on the ball. But Grandpa was right. It really helped."

Grandpa chuckled. "The boy got real good at it. I just told him . . . use that talent, son, don't waste it. . . ."

Stick nodded. "When I'm upset, I give it up to the Lord and take my feelings out on the basketball court."

"Then you must have been upset a lot lately," Ruthie observed thoughtfully. "You could've beat those other teams single-handedly." She felt color flood her face at the first compliment she'd ever paid Stick.

He looked embarrassed and scuffed his shoe on the frayed carpet. "Nope, it's teamwork."

"The point is, Miss Ruthie," Grandpa said, rolling over to touch her arm as he talked, "don't be self-conscious. Be Christ-conscious. Think about Him while you're singing . . . give Him your problems . . . and everything will come out right."

"But it's so hard—" she began, but halted, seeing the spark in his eye. *Incredible!* she thought. *This man and I can communicate without words! I actually know what he's thinking! He's thinking how hard it is to sit in a wheelchair, completely dependent on other people, and give that to the Lord. But he's witnessing from that wheelchair anyway.*

"Thank you," she said, from the bottom of her heart. "Thank you, Grandpa."

Before they reached the street where Ruthie lived, it was snowing. "There's your snow, Nat." Awesome how God could translate what was happening in her spirit right now into that fresh blanket of white falling on Garden City.

Stephanie rummaged through her purse. "Give this to Justin, will you?"

It was a picture of Stick in his wise-man costume, with his hand on Justin's shoulder. Ruthie didn't think she'd ever see Stick as "the class clown" anymore. Guess she wouldn't think of him as a boy, either. Strange, this afternoon he seemed to have become a "wise man" named Aric.

After Natalie dropped her off, saying she needed to spend some time with Scott, Ruthie told her mom what had happened at Stick's place. And as soon as she was in her room alone, with Justin tucked in for the night, she got on her knees and poured out her thanks to the Lord, holding on to the little white dove on the chain around her neck.

"Thank you, God, for this reminder of the greatness of your Spirit. Thank you for letting me see it in Stick's family. Thank you for giving me a new Grandpa, who showed me what you're like. I'm giving my problems to you, Lord. And in case he doesn't know how to, I'm giving *Sean's* problems to you, too. I trust you to know what's best for both of us, since neither of us has a clue.

"Forgive me when I fail. My throat has been so choked up lately. Just help me not to cave in tomorrow but to remember that my talent comes from you. And if Sean makes it to the pageant, carry your message through the music—straight to his heart. Help me not to think of myself—only you. . . ."

The "amen" just wouldn't come because the prayer wasn't over. Cleansing tears flowed until Ruthie felt drained of all her worries. Now God could fill her with His peace and love. . . .

Christmas Day dawned bright and beautiful—and *white*.

The living room floor was already littered with Christmas wrapping and ribbons. Justin had rousted them out of bed at 4:30 A.M. "to see if my new snake is in one of those neat packages."

When the phone rang, Ruthie almost allowed herself to hope it could be Sean, then shook off the thought. Sean was a closed chapter in her life.

It was Rose Ainsworth, instead, asking if Ruthie and Justin could come over.

"We thought it was important that your little brother be in on our Christmas morning devotions this year," Mr. A. explained to Ruthie when she drove Justin over after breakfast.

The entire family—Jim and Jill Ainsworth and their four daughters—were all gathered in the living room near the Christmas tree. Natalie patted a spot for Ruthie on the sofa beside her.

Rose jumped up to greet Justin. "Here," she said,

handing him a small figure of the Baby Jesus. "*You* do it . . . when Daddy gets to that part of the story."

Justin turned pale, and Ruthie put a reassuring hand on his shoulder, her fingers trailing down over his chest. She could feel his heart hammering like a drum. Was he nervous? Or scared?

"This is the whole reason we celebrate Christmas," Mr. A. began, flipping the pages of his Bible to the passage in Luke: " 'And it came to pass in those days, that there went out a decree from Caesar Augustus, that all the world should be taxed. . . . ' "

There was not a sound as he continued reading the familiar story of Mary and Joseph making the long trip to the city of David, where they found huge crowds of people who had come from near and far to be taxed. Mary, in an advanced state of her pregnancy, must have been exhausted. And Joseph evidently hadn't made reservations, for the story went on: " 'And she brought forth her firstborn son, and wrapped him in swaddling clothes, and laid him in a manger; because there was no room for them in the inn. . . . ' "

At a nod from Mr. A., Justin rose and walked stiffly, as if he were carrying a fragile piece of glass that would shatter if he tripped. Very carefully he laid the Baby Jesus in the makeshift manger, then breathed a huge sigh of relief and lifted his fists above his head. "Yes!"

The sanctuary was packed when Ruthie filed into the choir loft with the others on Christmas night and looked out over the crowd. Seated down front—with Nat and Scott and the Ainsworths—were Cissy and

Antonio and her parents. Right behind them were Mom, Dad, and Justin, clutching his new stuffed boa constrictor and grinning up at her.

Over to the left, she spotted Stick and his mom . . . and in the aisle beside them was Grandpa in his wheelchair. The old man flashed her a tilted smile and a shaky thumbs-up. She smiled back, feeling better already.

There wasn't time to check the balcony, but so far, she hadn't seen a sign of Sean. Maybe he'd slip in late and sit at the back. But at that moment, the pastor stepped forward to say a few words, and there wasn't time to wonder.

"What better time than this day on which we celebrate Christ's birth to accept Him as your own personal Savior—the One who came as a baby to die for your sins? Think about that as you hear the glorious music of this holy season." He nodded to the choir director and took a seat in the front row.

As the violinists played the opening measures, music filled the sanctuary, and Ruthie was sure her heart would burst with joy. In song after song, her voice joined all the others in praise to the newborn King.

The chord for the final number came before she knew it. The big finish, when she would sing her solo— if she could pull it off. Ruthie closed her eyes—choosing to shut out the faces of the audience down front and focus on the face of the One whose birthday they were celebrating.

Her first notes sounded—breathy and hesitant. "O holy night, the stars are brightly shining—it is the night of the dear Savior's birth. . . ."

As she sang, her voice gained strength, and she hardly knew she was singing—only that the words flowed from her heart freely, rising in a gift of love to God's Son.

"Fall on your knees; O hear the angel voices. O night divine . . . O night, when Christ was born. . . ."

The last notes soared steadily—high, higher, and still higher—above the heads of the congregation, past the balcony, and out through the stained-glass windows into the heavens. There was no fear that her voice might break on the last high note: "O night divi-ine, O night when Christ was born."

The song ended, and there was a hush over the audience. Ruthie opened her eyes, feeling a peace she'd never experienced before. She barely registered the fact that Pastor Ward was standing down front, with his hand stretched out to receive someone, the pastor's body blocking the person from view.

"We've had one come tonight, wanting to give his heart and life to the Lord Jesus. Let's pray for him and for ourselves that all of us will be the right example as he grows in Christ."

When he stepped aside, Ruthie gasped. It was not Sean standing there with Pastor Ward, as she'd secretly hoped for a fraction of a second, but Justin! Her own little brother!

The following Sunday, Ruthie still hadn't heard from Sean. But she sat with her dad and mom in church, watching Justin's baptism.

As Pastor Ward gently lowered her brother into the

water, then lifted him up, water streaming from his coppery curls, Ruthie was reminded of how beautifully that action symbolized how one "died" to self and sin and rose to begin a whole new life.

She felt a surge of hope in her heart. If Justin, who had given her the credit for helping him see that Baby Jesus really belonged in his *heart* and not just in a manger, then maybe she could still get through to Sean.

After the service, she walked outside the church, seeing that the low-hanging clouds had again released their heavy burden and were covering the landscape with a pure white blanket.

I've let go, too, she thought. *Just as my little brother is beginning a new life with the Lord, so am I.*

She looked up into the sky, feeling the soft flakes kissing her cheeks. *Thanks, Lord, for this new life you've given Justin . . . and for giving me another chance. . . .*

Can Ruthie resist Sean's determination to win her back? And is his resolve strong enough to keep him out of trouble?

Natalie, with her faith and common-sense approach to things, can help—but where *is* Nat? And where is the inmate who has recently escaped from the federal prison?

Hampering the search efforts is the torrential rain, dumping tons of water on southern Illinois and flooding low-lying areas. Will they find the escapee—and Natalie—before it's too late?

Watch to see how this tense situation affects the future plans of all concerned . . . in WHITE DOVE ROMANCE #6.

Teen Series From Bethany House Publishers

Early Teen Fiction (11–14)

HIGH HURDLES by Lauraine Snelling
Show jumper DJ Randall strives to defy the odds and achieve her dream of winning Olympic Gold.

SUMMERHILL SECRETS by Beverly Lewis
Fun-loving Merry Hanson encounters mystery and excitement in Pennsylvania's Amish country.

THE TIME NAVIGATORS by Gilbert Morris
Travel back in time with Danny and Dixie as they explore unforgettable moments in history.

Young Adult Fiction (12 and up)

CEDAR RIVER DAYDREAMS by Judy Baer
Experience the challenges and excitement of high school life with Lexi Leighton and her friends—over one million books sold!

GOLDEN FILLY SERIES by Lauraine Snelling
Readers are in for an exhilarating ride as Tricia Evanston races to become the first female jockey to win the sought-after Triple Crown.

JENNIE MCGRADY MYSTERIES by Patricia Rushford
A contemporary Nancy Drew, Jennie McGrady's sleuthing talents promise to keep readers on the edge of their seats.

LIVE! FROM BRENTWOOD HIGH by Judy Baer
When eight teenagers invade the newsroom, the result is an action-packed teen-run news show exploring the love, laughter, and tears of high school life.

THE SPECTRUM CHRONICLES by Thomas Locke
Adventure and romance await readers in this fantasy series set in another place and time.

SPRINGSONG BOOKS by various authors
Compelling love stories and contemporary themes promise to capture the hearts of readers.

WHITE DOVE ROMANCES by Yvonne Lehman
Romance, suspense, and fast-paced action for teens committed to finding pure love.